The Sorrows of
Young Werther

The Sorrows of
Young Werther

Johann Wolfgang von Goethe

Translated by

Bayard Quincy Morgan

ONEWORLD
CLASSICS

ONEWORLD CLASSICS LTD
London House
243-253 Lower Mortlake Road
Richmond
Surrey TW9 2LL
United Kingdom
www.oneworldclassics.com

Die Leiden des jungen Werther first published in 1774
This translation first published under the title *The Sufferings of Young Werther* by John Calder (Publishers) Ltd in 1957
This revised edition first published by Oneworld Classics Limited in 2010
English translation and Introduction © Oneworld Classics, 1957, 2010
Reprinted 2011

Printed in Great Britain by CPI Cox & Wyman, Reading

ISBN: 978-1-84749-157-2

Contents

Introduction

O N 30TH OCTOBER 1772, Legation Secretary Karl Wilhelm Jerusalem in Wetzlar shot and killed himself with a pistol borrowed from J.C. Kestner, a friend of Goethe. Jerusalem was Goethe's friend too; he had first met Goethe, who was two years his junior, as a student in Leipzig, and their association had been renewed that summer in Wetzlar. The tragedy made a profound impression on Goethe, and I see in *The Sorrows of Young Werther* a certain vindication of his friend (what his contemporary Lessing might have termed a *Rettung*, i.e., a rescue from misjudgement). Jerusalem's death must have been discussed with animation and some heat, and much of what Goethe put into Werther's letter of 12th August 1771 was no doubt a digest of arguments which he had himself used in trying to explain, if not to justify, Jerusalem's act. I think even the hero's name may be significant, for in German the word *wert* (old spelling *werth*) means "worthy, estimable".

Not a little of Werther's story derives from Jerusalem: his dislike of official conventionality (24th December 1771), his annoyance at verbal pedantry (*ibid.*), his aversion to the Ambassador (17th February 1772), his wounded feelings at being snubbed by aristocrats (16th March 1772) and his unhappy (and unrequited) love for a married woman (whose husband threw him out). The rest is largely supplied by young Goethe himself, who in his passionate attachment to Charlotte Buff, later the wife of Kestner, wrote letters just like Werther's. It will be noted that Werther's birthday is the same as Goethe's (28th August 1771); quite Goethean is his rapturous delight in nature; his admiration for Homer; his pantheism (letter of 18th August). As to Werther's suicide, we may confidently assume that Goethe had entertained thoughts of ending his life at times when overmastering emotion resulted in feelings of frustration and defeat.

The result of this combination of actualities was a milestone in German literature. *Werther* is the first German novelette (a form in which German writers have excelled), the first German epistolary novel and the first German work of any kind to make both its author and his country's literature internationally known. Translations appeared promptly in France and England, where twenty-six separate editions (of a translation from the French) were published up to 1800. No less a realist than Napoleon was a great admirer of the story, which he is said to have read seven times, and which he discussed with Goethe when they met in 1808. In Germany the work created a tremendous sensation: within twelve years after its first publication twenty unauthorized editions had been issued. The "Werther costume", consisting of blue tailed coat, yellow waistcoat and trousers with high boots (16th September 1772), was adopted everywhere and was worn at Weimar by the court when Goethe went there in 1775.

We need to recall such facts when we approach a story which is in many respects so foreign to our present modes of thought and expression. Young men today, however greatly they may be influenced by emotion, do not shed "a thousand tears" or impress "a thousand kisses" on a lady's picture. But this is the way the eighteenth century talked, the way it liked to think that a lover's devotion should express itself. No single work can communicate to us as authentically as *Werther* the extravagances of feeling and utterance which mark the trend in German letters commonly designated as "Storm and Stress", a trend which was the precursor of the Romanticism that took the lead in German literature at the turn of the century and kept it for more than thirty years.

At the same time, *Werther* is the first psychological novel in German. There are few actual happenings, and what we experience, with extraordinary clarity and vividness, is the drama which runs its course in the mind and heart of the hero. Considering Goethe's self-imposed limitation – there are no replies to Werther's letters – it was a *tour de force* hardly equalled in Western literature to make the reader inhabit Werther's soul, as it were, without any flagging of interest and even with peaks of considerable excitement.

A special note on Ossian seems in order, since today the Ossianic poems are probably deader than any other item in eighteenth-century literature. We need to remind ourselves that when Goethe wrote *Werther,* Macpherson's fake had not been disclosed, and that his sentimental fabrications were believed to represent a genuine, wild primitivity. Hence the vogue of Ossian can make a signal contribution to our understanding of eighteenth-century mentality and aid in the correct assessment of *Werther* itself. Knowing that Werther's feeling towards Ossian was actually Goethe's, we can better appreciate the artistic purpose underlying the introduction of a lengthy quotation from Ossian (in Goethe's own translation). It was necessary, he saw, that Lotte should be moved to the depths, lifted out of herself and thus prepared to be overcome by Werther's outburst of passion; to achieve this, she had to be withdrawn from her own everyday world and immersed in a wholly different one, in which she should be bathed in beautiful diction, saturated with sentiment. Assuming her (and the reader's) enthusiasm for Ossian, this was the perfect agency for Goethe to employ. The *matter* of the long quotation is of little moment: Goethe wanted merely the emotional build-up. What serves them as catalyst is the short passage (remote in Ossian from the previous one, and slightly altered in Goethe's version) in which the singer foretells his own death; Werther, by now in a state of the utmost turmoil, cannot fail to break down at this point, and that in turn brings on a crisis which makes his suicide inevitable.

So great was Goethe's success in bringing Werther to life, so deep was the sympathy he evoked for him, that he was thought by many to have put the stamp of his approval on

Werther's character, and moreover to have written a defence of human suicide. As to this, it need only be remarked that Shakespeare could make Hamlet understandable without sharing his views or living his life. The mere fact that young Goethe did not take his own life, for all his tempestuous nature and his passionate grief over Lotte Buff, is sufficient evidence that he intended Werther's suicide to be understood as the necessary culmination of a course of action which was itself not necessary, although humanly understandable.

It is interesting that Werther-Goethe discovered a principle (15th August 1771) which Rudyard Kipling was to put into practice in his *Just so Stories*. And it is amusing to find Werther advising a poet to let his own work alone; for Goethe did not take his hero's advice. Originally dashed off in 1774 in a veritable fever of creativeness, *Werther* was thoughtfully revised in the years 1783–86, the most substantial addition to the letters themselves being the episode of the servant in love with his employer (30th May 1771), who finally murders his rival. The other important change was a marked enlargement (about fifty per cent) of the epilogue written by the "editor". It is however noteworthy – and to that extent Goethe did abide by his own prescription – that not only the basic substance of the story remained unaltered, but that even its external form was not tampered with. Goethe did not rewrite *Werther*, he merely saw to it that his original intent should be even more effectively carried out than in the first version.

Werther remains, then, along with the *Urfaust* and some deathless poems, as the literary monument which young Goethe erected to himself and to the people from which he sprang. As long as German literature of the eighteenth century is studied, *Werther* must be included.

– Bayard Quincy Morgan

Chronology

1749   Born at Frankfurt-am-Main.

1765–68   Studied at Leipzig.

1770–71   Studied law at Strasburg.

1772   Spent some months in Wetzlar at the Supreme Court of the Empire.

1773   *Götz von Berlichingen* (prose drama).

1774   *Clavigo* (prose drama).

1774   *Die Leiden des jungen Werther* (novel; rev. 1783–86).

1775   *Stella* (prose drama).

1775   Invited to Weimar as companion to young duke, remained there.

1776–85   *Wilhelm Meisters theatralische Sendung* (novel).

1779   *Iphigenie auf Tauris* (prose drama; changed to blank verse in 1787).

1781   *Torquato Tasso* (verse drama; completed 1789).

1786–88   Journey to Italy, sojourn in Rome.

1787   *Egmont* (prose drama).

1790   *Faust (Fragment)* (verse drama).

1794   *Reineke Fuchs* (verse epic).

1795–96   *Wilhelm Meisters Lehrjahre* (novel, revision of the *Sendung*).

1797   *Hermann und Dorothea* (verse epic).

1797–99   *Achilleis* (unfinished verse epic).

1803   *Die natürliche Tochter* (verse drama).

1808   *Faust, erster Teil* (verse drama).

1808   *Pandora* (masque in verse).

1809   *Die Wahlverwandtschaften* (novel).
1809   *Farbenlehre* (theory of optics).
1811–   *Dichtung und Wahrheit* (autobiography).
1819   *Der west-östliche Divan* (poems).
1829   *Wilhelm Meisters Wanderjahre* (novel).
1831   *Faust, zweiter Teil* (verse drama, printed post-humously).
1832   Death of Goethe.

The Sorrows of
Young Werther

I HAVE CAREFULLY COLLECTED all I could possibly find out about the history of poor Werther, and I lay it before you here, knowing that you will thank me for doing so. You cannot deny his mind and character your admiration and love, or his fate your tears.

And you, good soul, who are feeling the same anguish as he, draw consolation from his sufferings, and let this little book be your friend, if fate or your own fault prevent you from finding a closer one.

First Book

4th May 1771

How happy I am to be gone! Best of friends, what is the heart of man! To forsake you, whom I love so much, from whom I was inseparable, and be happy! I know you will forgive me for it. Were not my other associations so chosen by Fate as to make a heart like mine uneasy? Poor Leonore! And yet it was not my fault. Could I help it that while the compelling charms of her sister gave me agreeable entertainment, that poor heart developed its own passion? And yet – am I quite without fault? Did I not nourish her feelings? Did I not myself delight in those wholly authentic manifestations of nature which so often made us laugh, little laughable as they were? Did I not – O what is man, that he has a right to lament what he is? I will, dear friend, I promise you, I will reform, will no longer harp on the misfortunes with which fate presents us, as I have always done; I will enjoy the present, and the past shall be past. You are certainly right, best of men: there would be fewer sufferings among men if they did not – God knows why they are so made – so industriously employ their imagination in recalling the memories of past evils, rather than endure a colourless present.

Please be so good as to tell my mother that I shall attend to her affair as best I can and send her a report of it as soon as possible. I have seen my aunt and find her far from being the vixen that people at home make of her. She is a lively, impetuous woman with the best of hearts. I explained to her my mother's complaints regarding that portion of the inheritance which has been withheld; she gave me her reasons and the facts, and named the conditions under which she would be ready to hand over everything, and even more than we demanded – in short, I don't care to write about it now, but tell my mother that everything will be all right. And in connection with this little matter I have again found, my dear fellow, that misunderstandings and lethargy perhaps produce more wrong in the world than deceit and malice do. At least the two latter are certainly rarer.

For the rest, I like it here very much. Solitude in this paradise is a precious balm to my heart, and this youthful time of year warms with all its fullness my oft-shivering heart. Every tree, every hedge is a bouquet of flowers, and one would like to turn into a cockchafer, to be able to float about in this sea of scents and find all one's nourishment in it.

The town itself is unpleasant, but on the other hand all around it lies inexpressibly beautiful nature. It was this which induced the late Count M. to lay out a garden on one of the hills which intersect with the most charming diversity, forming the loveliest valleys. The garden is unpretentious, and you no sooner enter it than you feel that it was designed not by a scientific gardener but by a man with a sensitive heart, who wanted to use it for the enjoyment of himself. I have already shed many a tear for the deceased in the decayed little bower which was his favourite spot and is now mine. Soon I shall be the master of the garden; the gardener has a liking for me, even after so few days, and he will not suffer by it.

10th May

A wonderful cheerfulness has taken possession of my whole soul, similar to the sweet spring mornings which I enjoy with all my heart. I am alone and glad to be alive in this locality, which was created for such souls as mine. I am so happy, dear friend, so completely immersed in the realization of a tranquil existence, that my art is suffering neglect. I could not draw at all now, not a line, and yet I have never been a greater painter than I am now. When the beloved valley steams around me, and the lofty sun rests on the surface of the impenetrable darkness of my forest with only single rays stealing into the inner sanctuary, then I lie in the tall grass beside the murmuring brook, while on the earth near me a thousand varied grasses strike me as significant; when I feel the swarming life of the little world between the grass blades, the innumerable, unfathomable shapes of the tiny worms and flies, closer to my heart, and feel the presence of the Almighty, who created us in his image, feel the breath of the all-loving one, who, afloat in eternal rapture, bears and sustains us – O my friend! – then when twilight invests my eyes, and the world about me and the heaven above me rests wholly in my soul like the image of a woman one loves – then I am often all longing and I think: ah, could you express all that again, could you breathe onto paper that which lives in you so fully, so warmly, so that it would become the reflection of your soul, as your soul is a mirror of the infinite God! My friend – but this experience is beyond my strength, I succumb to the overpowering glory of what I behold.

12th May

I don't know whether deluding spirits hover about this region, or whether it is the warm, heavenly fancy in my heart which turns my whole environment into a paradise. Thus, directly outside the town there is a well, one to which I am magically bound like Melusine and her sisters.* You go down a little slope and find yourself in front of a vault in which about twenty steps descend to a spot where the clearest water gushes out of marble rocks. The little wall which serves as coping at the top, the tall trees which give shade all around, the coolness of the spot – all this has a suggestive, mysterious character. Not a day passes without my sitting there for an hour. Then the maids come from the town and fetch water, the most innocent and necessary of employments, which in former days the daughters of kings engaged in themselves. When I sit there, the patriarchal idea is vividly realized about me, as all the men of old make friends or go courting at the well, while beneficent spirits hover about the wellsprings and fountains. Oh, a man who cannot share that experience must never have been refreshed, after an arduous journey in the summer, by the coolness of a wellspring.

13th May

You ask whether to send me my books – friend, I beg you for the love of God, don't load me up with them! I do not wish to be guided, encouraged, enkindled any more; my heart effervesces enough all by itself. What I need is lullabies, and I have found an abundance of them in my Homer. How often do I lull my agitated blood into quiet, for you have never seen anything as uneven, as unstable, as this heart. Good friend, do I need to tell that to you, who have so often borne the burden of seeing me pass from grief to extravagant joy and from sweet melancholy to disastrous passion? Moreover, I treat my heart like a sick child, granting its every wish. Do not pass this on; there are those who would reproach me for it.

15th May

The lower classes here know me already and love me, especially the children. When I sought their acquaintance to begin with, and put friendly questions to them about this and that, some of them thought I was making fun of them and snubbed me quite rudely. I did not let this bother me; I only felt most keenly what I have often observed before: people of some rank will always keep the common people coolly at a distance, as if they thought they would lose something by approaching them, and then too there are social apostates and practical jokers, who seem to condescend, making their arrogance all the more painful to the poor.

I am quite aware that we are not equal and cannot be equal, but I hold that he who thinks it necessary to withdraw from the so-called rabble in order to keep their respect is just as reprehensible as a coward who hides from his enemy because he is afraid of defeat.

Recently, as I came to the spring, I found a young servant girl who had put her pitcher on the lowest step and was looking around to see if no fellow servant were coming along to help her get it on her head. I descended and looked at her. "Shall I help you, girl?" said I. She blushed up to her ears. "Oh no, sir!" she said. "Don't stand on ceremony." She adjusted her head cushion, and I helped her. She thanked me and mounted the steps.

17th May

I have made all kinds of acquaintances, but so far I have not found any companions. I don't know, something about me must attract people; so many of them like me and cling to me, and it pains me when our common journey takes us only a short distance. If you ask what the people here are like, I must tell you, "Like people everywhere!" Uniformity marks the human race. Most of them spend the greater part of their time in working for a living, and the scanty freedom that is left to them burdens them so that they seek every means of getting rid of it. O fate of man!

But these people are a very good sort! If I forget myself once in a while, tasting with them the joys that are still granted to me, such as exchanging pleasantries in all candour and ingenuousness around a prettily set table, planning an excursion, or arranging for a well-timed dance, and the like, the effect on me is very good; only I must not let myself think that in me lie ever so many other powers, all of which moulder for lack of use, and which I must carefully conceal. Ah, and that fetters my whole heart – and yet! To be misunderstood is the fate of such as I.

Alas that the friend of my youth is gone! Alas that I ever knew her! I could say, "You are a fool! For you are seeking what is not to be found here below!" But I did have her friendship, I sensed that heart, that great soul, in whose presence I felt myself to be more than I was, because I was all that I could be. Good God! Was there a single force in my soul which remained unused? Could I not, when with her, unfold that entire power of feeling with which my heart embraces all nature? Was not our association an endless play of the subtlest feeling, of the keenest wit, a wit whose variations, not excluding some flippancy, bore the stamp of genius? And now! Ah, the years of hers which exceeded mine brought her before me to the grave. Never shall I forget her, never her steadfast mind and her divine indulgence.

A few days ago I met a young man named V., an ingenuous youth with a very happy physiognomy. He has just come from the university, and though he does not exactly think himself wise, he does believe he knows more than others. He was diligent too, as I can tell in all sorts of ways – in short, he is pretty well informed. Having heard that I draw a great deal and know Greek (two rare phenomena in these skies), he sought me out and unloaded much learning, from Batteux to Robert Wood, from Roger de Piles to Winckelmann, assuring me that he had read Sulzer's *General Theory of the Fine Arts*, that is, the first part of it, from beginning to end, and that he owned a MS of Heyne on the study of classical antiquity.* I let it go at that.

Furthermore, I have made the acquaintance of a very fine person: a steward of the prince, a frank and ingenuous man. They say it rejoices the soul to see him in the midst of his children, of whom he has nine; in particular they make a great fuss over his eldest daughter. He has invited me to his house, and I will call on him one of these days. He is living in one of the prince's hunting lodges, an hour and a half from here on foot, having received permission to move there after the death of his wife, since he found residence here in the town and in the official dwelling too painful.

In addition, a number of eccentric freaks have crossed my path whom I find insufferable in every respect, most unendurable being their manifestations of friendship.

Farewell! This letter will suit you, for it is nothing but a report.

22nd May

That the life of man is only a dream has seemed to be so to many before now, and I too always carry this feeling about with me. When I behold the narrow bounds which confine man's powers of action and investigation; when I see how all his efficiency aims at the satisfaction of needs which in their turn have no purpose save to prolong our unhappy existence, and then see that all our reassurance regarding certain matters of inquiry is merely a resigned kind of dreaming, whereby we paint the walls within which we are confined with cheerful figures and bright prospects – all this, Wilhelm, forces me into silence. I return into myself, and find a world! But again a world of groping and vague desires rather than one of clear delineation and active force. And then everything grows hazy to my senses, and in a sort of dream I keep on smiling at the world.

All learned schoolmasters and educators agree that children do not know why they want what they want, but that adults too, as well as children, stagger around on this earth, like them not knowing whence they come and whither they go, pursue true goals just as little as they, and are just as completely governed by biscuits and cakes and birch rods: nobody will believe that, and yet it seems to me palpable.

I am ready to grant – for I know what you would say to this – that the happiest are those who like children live for the day, drag their dolls around, dressing and undressing them, slink with bated breath about the drawer where Mama keeps the sweets locked up and, when they finally get hold of what they want, gobble it down by the mouthful and cry, "More!" – those are happy creatures. Happy are those too who give sumptuous titles to their shabby occupations, perhaps even to their passions, recommending them to the human race as gigantic operations contributing to man's salvation and welfare. Happy the man who can be like that! But one who recognizes in all humility what all this comes to, who sees how amiably every happy citizen manages to shape his little garden into a paradise, and how indefatigably even the unhappy man plods along panting under his burden, while all of them take the same interest in having one more minute to see the light of this sun – ah, he holds his peace, and he too creates his world in himself, and is moreover happy because he is a human being. And then, confined and fettered as he is, still he continues to keep in his heart the sweet feeling of freedom, knowing that he can quit this prison whenever he will.

26th May

You have long known my way of settling down, pitching my tent in some spot I like, and lodging there in a modest fashion. Here too I have again come upon a nook that I found attractive.

About an hour's walk from town lies a place called Wahlheim.* Its situation on a hill is very interesting, and when you leave the village on the upper footpath, all at once you are overlooking the entire valley. A good-hearted hostess, who is obliging and lively for her age, dispenses wine, beer and coffee, and rising above everything else are two lindens whose spreading branches cover the small space before the church, which is completely ringed about with farmhouses, barns and courtyards. So private, so homelike a spot I have not readily found, and I have my little table carried out there from the inn, and my chair, and there I drink my coffee and read my Homer. The first time when I chanced to walk in under the lindens on a fine afternoon, I found the little spot so lonely. Everyone was in the fields, and only a boy of about four was sitting on the ground and holding close to his breast with both arms another one, perhaps half a year old, sitting between his feet, so that he made a kind of armchair for the baby and, for all the liveliness with which his black eyes looked about him, sat quite still. I found the sight charming: I sat down on a plough across the way and sketched this brotherly posture with great enjoyment. I added the nearest fence, a barn door and some broken wheels, all of it just as it stood there, and after the lapse of an hour I found that I had completed a well-disposed, very interesting drawing, without putting in the least imaginary detail. This strengthened me in my resolve to keep henceforth exclusively to nature. Nature alone is infinitely rich, and she alone forms the great artist. One can say much in favour of rules, about the same things as can be said in praise of civil society. A person who trains himself by the rules will never produce anything absurd or bad, just as one who lets himself be modelled after laws and decorum can never become an intolerable neighbour, never an outright villain; on the other hand any "rule", say what you like, will destroy the true feeling for nature and the true expression of her! I hear you say that that is too severe, that the rule merely restrains, prunes rank shoots, etc. – good friend, shall I give you a comparison? It may be likened to loving. A young heart is wholeheartedly bound up in a maiden, spends every daytime hour with her, squanders all its talents, all its fortune, in order to employ every moment in expressing its complete devotion to her. And now suppose some pedant comes along, a man who holds a public office, and says to him, "Fine young gentleman, to love is human, only you must be human in your loving! Apportion your hours, keeping some for work, and devote the hours of recreation to your maiden. Figure up your fortune, and whatever is in excess of your needs I will not forbid you to spend on a present for her, only not too often, say on her birthday or name day, etc." – if the youth obeys, then a useful young person will be the result, and I would even advise any prince to make him a counsellor; however, it will be the end of his love and, if he is an artist, of his art. O my friends! You ask why the stream of genius so seldom bursts forth, so seldom sends its sublime floods rushing in, to make your souls quake with astonishment? Dear friends, why, there along both banks of the river dwell the placid gentlemen whose summer houses, tulip beds and cabbage fields would be ruined, and who consequently manage to avert betimes, with dams and drainage ditches, any future threat.

27th May

I see that I have lapsed into raptures, parables and oratory, and have thus forgotten to complete the story of my further doings with the children. Wholly engrossed in the feelings of an artist, which my letter of yesterday presents to you in very fragmentary form, I sat on my plough for a good two hours. Then towards evening a young woman with a small basket on her arm came towards the children, who had not moved all this while, calling from a distance, "Philip, you're a good boy." She spoke to me, I thanked her, got up, approached her, and asked if she was the children's mother. She said yes and, giving the older one half a roll, she picked up the baby and kissed it with all a mother's love. "I told my Philip to hold the baby," said she, "and went into town with my oldest boy to get white bread and sugar, and an earthenware saucepan." I saw all this in the basket, the cover of which had fallen off. "I want to cook my Hans (that was the name of the youngest) a bit of soup for supper; the big boy, the scamp, broke my saucepan yesterday while quarrelling with Philip over the scrapings of the porridge." I asked about the oldest, and she had hardly told me that he was racing around the meadow with some geese when he came running and brought the second boy a hazel switch. I went on talking with the woman and learnt that she was the daughter of the schoolmaster, and that her husband had gone on a trip to Switzerland to get the legacy of a cousin. "They wanted to cheat him out of it," said she, "and didn't answer his letters; so he went there himself. I only hope

nothing has happened to him; I don't get any word from him."
I found it hard to part from the woman, but I gave each of the children a penny, and I gave her one for the youngest, so that she could bring him a roll to go with the soup as soon as she went into town, and so we separated.

I tell you, dear fellow, when my senses are strained to the limit, all the tumult within me is soothed by the sight of such a creature, who moves within the narrow round of her existence in happy tranquillity, gets along somehow from one day to the next and, seeing the leaves fall, is not moved to think anything but that winter is coming.

Since that day I have often been out there. The children are quite accustomed to me, they get sugar when I drink coffee, and in the evening they share bread and butter and clabber with me. On Sundays they never fail to get a penny, and if I am not there after prayer time, the hostess has orders to give it to them.

They feel confidential and tell me all sorts of things, and I delight especially in their passions and the simple expressions of their desires when a number of village children are assembled.

It has cost me much effort to rid the mother of her concern lest they should "incommode the gentleman".

30th May

What I recently told you about painting is certainly true of poetry as well; the only requirement is that one should recognize what is excellent and have the courage to express it, and that, to be sure, is saying much in few words. Today I experienced a scene which, written down as it was, would produce the finest idyll in the world, but of what use is poetry, scene and idyll? Must we always start tinkering when we are supposed to share in a phenomenon of nature?

If this introduction leads you to expect much that is lofty and distinguished, then you are once more badly deceived:

it is only a peasant lad who so carried me away that I took this lively interest. I shall tell it badly, as usual, and you will as usual, I imagine, think I am overdoing it; it is once more Wahlheim, and always Wahlheim, that produces these rarities.

There was a company outside under the lindens, drinking coffee. Because I did not altogether care for it, I lagged behind under some pretext.

A peasant lad came out of a neighbouring house and busied himself with the repair of some part of the plough which I had recently sketched. As I found him pleasing, I spoke to him, asked about his circumstances; we were soon acquainted and, as usually happens to me with this kind of people, soon on familiar terms. He told me that he was in the service of a widow, and very well treated by her. He told me so much about her, and praised her in such a way, that I could soon tell he was devoted to her, body and soul. She was no longer young, he said, she had been badly treated by her first husband and did not want to remarry, and from his narrative it was so shiningly evident how beautiful, how charming she seemed to him, and how greatly he wished that she might choose him, in order to wipe out the recollection of her first husband's faults, that I should have to repeat word for word to make you visualize the sheer affection, the love and loyalty of this man. Indeed, I should have to possess the gifts of the greatest poet in order to be able to give you at the same time a vivid depiction of the expressiveness of his gestures, the harmonious sound of his voice, the hidden fire of his glances. No, there are no words to express the gentleness which lay in his whole conduct and expression; anything I could reproduce would be merely clumsy. It touched me especially that he was so afraid I might have a wrong idea of his relation to her and have doubts of her good behaviour. How charming it was when he spoke of her figure, or her body which, without the charm of youth, attracted him powerfully and held him captive – I can only repeat that to myself in my inmost soul. In all my life I have not seen such urgent desire and ardent, intense yearning in such unmixed purity; indeed I can say that in such purity I have not imagined or dreamt it. Do not chide me when I say that the recollection of this genuine naturalness sets my inmost soul aglow, that the picture of this loyalty and tenderness follows me everywhere, and that I, as if set on fire by it, am languishing and pining.

I will now try to see her too in the near future, or rather, on further reflection, I will avoid that. It is better that I should see her through the eyes of her lover; perhaps she will not appear to my own eyes as she now stands before me, and why should I spoil that lovely picture?

16th June

Why I don't write to you? You ask that, and yet you too are one of those who are so learned. You should guess that I am doing fine, in fact – to sum it up, I have made an acquaintance which touches my heart closely. I have – I don't know.

To tell you step by step how it came about that I have learnt to know one of the most lovable of creatures will not be easy. I am happy and in high spirits, and that makes me a poor writer of history.

An angel – pshaw! That's what every man says of his sweetheart, isn't it? And yet I am not in a position to tell you in what respect she is perfect, why she is perfect; enough! She has taken possession of my whole being.

So much simplicity along with so much intelligence, so much kindness with so much firmness, tranquillity of soul and yet fully alive and active. All this is loathsome twaddle – what I am saying about her – pitiful abstractions, which do not express a single feature of her being. Another time – no, not another time, I'll tell you about it *now*. If I don't do it now, it would never happen. For, between us, since I began to write this, I was thrice on the point of laying down my pen, having my horse saddled and riding off. And yet I swore to myself this morning that I wouldn't ride out, and yet again I go to the window every other minute to see how high the sun still stands. I wasn't able to resist, I had to go out to see her. Here I am again, Wilhelm, I will sup on my bread and butter and write to you. What a rapture it is for my soul to see her in the midst of the lively, darling children, her eight brothers and sisters! If I continue like this, you'll be just as wise at the end as you were to start with. Listen then, I will force myself to go into detail.

I wrote you recently about having made the acquaintance of Bailiff S., and about his having invited me to visit him soon in his hermitage, or rather in his little kingdom. I neglected it, and perhaps I should never have gone out there if chance had not revealed to me the treasure which lies hidden in that quiet spot.

Our young people had arranged a dance out in the country, which I willingly agreed to attend. I offered to escort a nice, pretty, but otherwise commonplace local girl, and it was settled that I should hire a carriage, drive my partner and her cousin out to the place of festivities, and on the way stop to take Charlotte S. along. "You will get to know a beautiful woman," said my partner, as we rode through the clearing of the extensive forest towards the hunting lodge. "Be on your guard," added the cousin, "that you don't fall in love!" "Why?" said I. "She is already promised," was the reply, "to a very worthy man, who has gone out of town to arrange his affairs, because his father has died, and to apply for an important position." This information did not interest me much.

The sun was still a quarter of an hour above the mountains when we drove up before the courtyard gate. It was very sultry, and the ladies expressed their concern regarding a thunderstorm, which seemed to be gathering in grey-white, fleecy little clouds all around the horizon. I quieted their fears with a deceptive display of weather knowledge, although I myself began to suspect that our merry-making would get a jolt.

I alighted, and a maidservant who came to the gate begged us to wait a moment, saying that Miss Lottie would come soon. I walked through the courtyard towards the well-built house, and when I had mounted the outside steps, and stepped into the doorway, my eyes encountered the most charming spectacle I have ever seen. In the vestibule six children, ranging from eleven to two years old, were crowding round a beautifully formed girl of medium height, who was wearing a plain white dress with pale-pink bows on arm and breast. She was holding a loaf of black bread and cutting for the little ones around her slices appropriate to their age and appetite, and she handed over each one with such amiability, and each one called out its "Thank you!" so unaffectedly, stretching its little hands high into the air even before the slice was cut, and now either ran off delighted with its supper or, in accordance with its quieter temperament, walked tranquilly towards the gate, in order to see the strangers, and the carriage in which their Lottie was to ride away. "I beg pardon," she said, "for making you come in and letting the ladies wait. What with dressing, and giving all kinds of directions regarding the house during my absence, I forgot to give the children their supper, and they won't have anyone cut bread for them but me."

I paid her some indifferent compliment, for my whole soul was fixed upon her figure, her tone of voice, her whole behaviour, and I barely had time to recover from my surprise while she ran into the living room to get her gloves and her fan. The little ones were looking askance at me from some distance, and I walked up to the youngest one, a child with the most attractive face. He was drawing back just as Lotte came out of the door and said, "Louis, shake hands with our cousin." The boy did that very readily, and I could not refrain from kissing him heartily, regardless of his runny nose.

"Cousin?" said I, extending my hand to her. "Do you think I am worthy of the happiness of being related to you?"

"Oh," said she with an easy smile, "our relationship is very extensive, and I should be sorry if you were the worst among them." As she went, she gave Sophie, her next oldest sister, a girl of about eleven, instructions to keep good watch over the children, and to say hello to Papa when he came home from his pleasure ride. She told the little ones to obey their sister Sophie as if Sophie were she, and some of them promised this expressly. But a pert little girl of about six said, "All the same, Lottie, she isn't you, and we like you better." The two oldest boys had climbed up onto the back of the carriage, and at my request she gave them permission to ride along to the edge of the forest, if they would promise not to annoy each other, and to hold on tight.

We had scarcely got properly seated, the ladies having greeted each other, with alternate comments on each other's dresses and especially their hats, and having given the company they expected to find a thorough going-over, when Lotte bade the driver stop and let her brothers get down; they insisted on kissing her hand again, which the oldest did with all the tenderness appropriate to his fifteen years, the other with much impetuosity and frivolity. She sent her love to the little ones again, and we drove on.

The cousin asked if she had done with the book she had recently sent her. "No," said Lotte, "I don't like it, you can have it back. And the one before that was no better." I was astonished when, on my asking what the books were, she answered...* I found so much personality in all that she said, and every word showed me new charms, new rays of intellect bursting forth from her face, which seemed little by little to blossom out with pleasure, because she could feel by my bearing that I understood her.

"When I was younger," she said, "I liked nothing so much as novels. God knows how content I was when on a Sunday I could just settle into a corner, to participate with all my heart in the fortune and misfortune of some Miss Jenny. Nor do I deny that such reading still has some charm for me, but since I so rarely have time to read a book, it must be something that just suits my taste. And that author is my favourite in whom I find my own world again, in whose work life goes on like my own, and yet whose story becomes as interesting and as heartfelt as my own domestic life, which to be sure is no paradise, but still on the whole a source of unspeakable happiness."

I strove to conceal the agitation which these words produced in me. This did not do much good, to be sure; for when I heard her in passing speak with such truth about *The Vicar of Wakefield*, about...* I was soon beside myself, told her everything I could not help saying, and only observed after some time, when Lotte shifted the conversation to take in the others, that they had sat there wide-eyed the whole time, as if they were not present. The cousin looked at me more than once with a mocking upturn of her nose, which however mattered nothing to me.

The conversation took up the pleasure of dancing. "If this passion is a fault," said Lotte, "I readily admit nevertheless that I know nothing to surpass dancing. And if anything troubles me and I hammer out a quadrille on my old piano, out of tune as it is, that makes everything all right again."

How I feasted on her black eyes during this conversation! How the vivacious lips and the fresh, hearty cheeks drew to them my whole soul! How I, wholly absorbed in the glorious ideas she was expressing, often failed completely to hear the words with which she conveyed her meaning! You have some picture of that, because you know me. In short, I got out of the carriage as if dreaming, when we came to a halt before the pavilion, and was so lost in dreams, in the twilit world around me, that I scarcely gave a thought to the music which flooded down towards us from the illuminated ballroom.

The two gentlemen who were the partners of the cousin and Lotte, Mr Audran and a certain N.N. – who can remember all the names? – met us at the carriage, took charge of their ladies, and I escorted my partner upstairs.

We wound around each other in minuets; I claimed one lady after another, and it was just the most unattractive ones who could not manage to clasp one's hand and make an end. Lotte and her partner began an English square dance, and you can appreciate how happy I felt when in due course she began to dance the figure with us. One must *see* her dance! You see, she is so wrapped up in it with her whole heart and her whole soul, her whole body one single harmony, so carefree, so unaffected, as if the dance were really everything, as if she were thinking nothing else, feeling nothing else; and in that moment, surely, everything else fades away.

I asked for the second quadrille; she promised me the third, and with the most amiable ingenuousness in the world she assured me that she loved the German style of dancing. "It is the fashion here," she went on, "for every couple that belong together to stay together during the German dance, and my partner is a poor waltzer and will thank me if I spare him the trouble. Your lady can't waltz either, and doesn't like to, and during the quadrille I saw that you waltz well; now if you will be mine for the German dance, then go and request it of my gentleman, and I will talk to your lady." I shook hands on it, and we agreed that during that time her partner should entertain mine.

Now the dance began, and for a while we took pleasure in interlacing our arms in various ways. With what charm, with what fleetness she moved! And now when it actually came to waltzing, and we revolved about each other like the spheres, at first there was a little confusion, to be sure, because very few are skilled at it. We were astute and let them romp their fill, and when the clumsiest couples had quit the field, we swung in and held out valiantly with one other couple, Audran and his partner. Never have I been so light on my feet. I was no longer human. To hold in my arms the most lovable creature, and flying about with her like lightning, so that everything about me faded away, and – to be honest, Wilhelm, I did swear to myself all the same that a girl I loved and had a claim upon should never waltz with anyone but me, and even if I lost my life over it. You know what I mean!

We walked around the hall a few times to catch our breath. Then she sat down, and the oranges which I had previously put aside, and which by now were the only ones left, had an excellent effect, except that with every slice she handed to a demanding lady beside her for politeness's sake I felt a stab through my heart.

During the third quadrille we were the second couple. As we were going down the line, and I, clinging to her arm, was gazing with God knows how much rapture into her eyes, which were filled with the sincerest expression of the frankest, purest pleasure, we encounter a woman whom I had already observed because of the amiable effect of a face no longer young. She looks at Lotte with a smile, lifts a menacing finger, and as she speeds past us she says "Albert" twice in a very significant manner.

"Who is Albert?" said I to Lotte, "if it is not presumptuous to ask." She was on the point of answering when we had to separate in order to dance the big eight, and when our paths crossed it seemed to me that I detected a pensive cast on her brow. "Why should I deny it?" she said, as she gave me her hand for the promenade. "Albert is a fine person to whom I am as good as engaged." Now this was no news to me (for the girls had told me about it in the carriage), and yet it *was* utterly new to me, because I had not yet related it in my thoughts to her, who had become so dear to me in such a short time. Anyway, I got confused, forgot what I was doing, and danced in between the wrong couple, so that everything was at sixes and sevens, and it required all Lotte's presence of mind, with tugging and twisting, to restore order without loss of time.

The dance was not yet ended when the flashes which we had been seeing for some time along the horizon, and which I had steadily declared to be heat lightning, began to increase greatly, and the thunder drowned out the music. Three ladies ran out of the square, followed by their gentlemen; the disorder grew general, and the music stopped. It is natural that when a misfortune or something terrible surprises us in the midst of merriment, it makes a stronger impression on us than usual, partly on account of the contrast, which is so vividly experienced, partly and more so because our senses have become more perceptive and therefore receive an impression all the more rapidly. To such causes I must ascribe the extraordinary contortions into which I saw several ladies fall. The smartest one sat down in a corner with her back to the window and held her ears shut. Another knelt down before her and hid her head in the first one's lap. A third pushed in between the two and embraced her dear sisters, with endless tears. Some wanted to go home; others, who were still less aware of what they were doing, did not have enough presence of mind to stave off the importunities of some of our young fellows, who seemed to find an occupation in anticipating all the anxious prayers which were meant for Heaven, and in gathering them from the lips of the distressed beauties. Some of our gentlemen had gone below to smoke a pipe in peace, and the rest of the company raised no objection when the hostess hit upon the shrewd idea of putting at our disposal a room which had shutters and curtains. Scarcely had we got into it when Lotte busied herself with placing chairs in a circle and, when the company had sat down at her request, she proposed that they play a game.

I saw more than one purse up his lips and stretch his limbs in the hope of a juicy forfeit. "We'll play counting," she said. "Now pay attention! I will circle from right to left, and so you are to count in the same way, each saying his proper number, and that must go like wildfire, and whoever hesitates or makes a mistake gets a box on the ear, and so on up to a thousand." Now that was a merry sight. She walked around the circle with her arm outstretched. "One," said the first, his neighbour "Two", the next one "Three", and so on. Then she began to walk faster, and faster and faster; soon there was a mistake and slap! – went her hand, and the laughter confused the next one, and slap! And still faster. I myself got two slaps, and with keen pleasure I thought I observed that they were harder than the ones she usually dealt the others. Universal laughter and commotion ended the game before it had even got up to a thousand. The most intimate friends drew each other away, the storm was over, and I followed Lotte into the ballroom. As we went along, she said, "The ear-boxing made them forget the storm and everything!" I couldn't say a word. "I was one of the most timid," she continued, "and by pretending to be courageous in order to give the others courage I took heart myself." We stepped to the window. Off to one side there was thunder, and the splendid rain was trickling down upon the land; the most refreshing fragrance rose up to us from the rich abundance of the warm atmosphere. She stood leaning on her elbows, with her gaze searching the countryside; she looked up to heaven and at me; I saw her eyes fill with tears, and she laid her hand on mine, saying, "Klopstock!" I recalled at once the glorious ode* she had in mind, and became immersed in the stream of emotions which she had poured over me by uttering this symbolic name. I could not bear it, I bent down over her hand and kissed it amid tears of the utmost rapture. And looked into her eyes again – noble poet! Would that you had seen your apotheosis in that gaze, and would that your name, so often profaned, would never reach my ears from any other lips.

19th June

I no longer know where I stopped in my story the other day, but I know that it was two o'clock in the morning when I got to bed, and that if I could have chatted with you instead of writing, I might have kept you up until morning.

What happened on our return drive from the ball I haven't told you yet, and this is no day for it either.

It was the most glorious sunrise. The dripping woods, and the refreshed earth round about! Our other ladies fell into a doze. She asked me, didn't I want to join them? I shouldn't be uneasy on her account. "As long as I see those eyes open," I said, looking steadily at her, "there's no danger." And we both held out, all the way to her gate, which the maidservant quietly opened for her, assuring her in response to her questions that her father and the little ones were well, and all of them still asleep. Then I parted from her with the request that I might see her again that same day; she consented, and I went there; and since that time sun, moon and stars can calmly go about their business, but I am conscious neither of day nor night, and the whole world around me is fading away.

21st June

I am living through such happy days as God sets aside for his saints, and let become of me what will, I may never say that I have not tasted the joys, the unalloyed joys of life. You know my Wahlheim; there I am completely settled, from there it is only a half-hour's walk to Lotte, and there I feel all that I am and the full bliss that is given to man.

If I had thought, when I chose Wahlheim as the goal of my pleasure walks, that it was situated so close to heaven! How often, in the course of my lengthy wanderings, I have seen the hunting lodge, that embraces all my desires, now from the height, now from the plain across the river!

Dear Wilhelm, I have had all sorts of reflections concerning man's desire to expand, to make new discoveries, to rove about, and then again concerning his deep urge to accept willingly his confining limits, to drift along in the rut of habit, giving no heed to what lies either to right or left.

It is a wonder how, when I came here and looked down into the lovely valley from the hilltop, I was attracted by everything around me. That grove yonder! Oh, if I could mingle with its shade! That mountain top! Oh, if I could survey the broad expanse from there! Those hills linked together and the intimate valleys! Oh, if I could lose myself in them! I hastened thither, and I returned, and had not found what

I hoped. Ah, distance affects us like the future! Before our soul lies a vast, dimly outlined whole in which both feeling and sight lose themselves, and we yearn – ah! – to surrender our whole being, to let ourselves be filled with all the rapture of one great, glorious emotion. But alas! – when we hasten thither, when the There becomes the Here, everything is just as it was, and we stand there in our poverty, in our limitation, and our soul thirsts for refreshing water that has eluded us.

So it is that even the most restless rover finally longs for his native land, to find in his cottage, on the breast of his wife, in the circle of his children, in the affairs that furnish their support, the joy that he vainly sought in all the wide world.

When I walk out to my Wahlheim in the morning, at sunrise, and, having picked my own sugar peas in the garden of the inn, sit down and string them, reading now and then from my Homer, then when I select a pot in the little kitchen, dig out a piece of butter, put the pods on the flame, cover the pot, and sit down there so that I can shake them up occasionally – then I feel so vividly how Penelope's impudent suitors* slaughter oxen and swine, cut them up, and roast them. There is nothing that could fill me so completely with a quiet, genuine feeling as those traits of patriarchal life which I – thank God – can weave into my kind of life without affectation.

How fortunate it is for me that my heart can feel the plain, naive delight of the man who puts on the table a cabbage that he has grown himself, and for whom it is not merely the vegetable – but all the good days, the fine morning when he planted it, the pleasant evenings when he watered it, taking his pleasure in its thriving growth – that he enjoys again in one comprehensive moment.

29th June

The day before yesterday the town doctor came out to see the steward and found me on the floor among Lotte's children, some of them scrambling over me, others teasing me, while I tickled them and provoked a great outcry on their part. The doctor, who is a very dogmatic puppet, smooths the folds of his cuffs while talking, and pulls out a shirt frill that has no end, considered this to be beneath the dignity of an intelligent person; I could tell by the tilt of his nose. But I paid not the least attention, let him discourse on very sensible matters, and rebuilt for the children the card houses they had knocked down. This also led to his going about town and complaining that the steward's children were spoilt enough as it was, but Werther was now ruining them completely.

Yes, dear Wilhelm, of all living things on earth, children are closest to my heart. When I watch them, and see in the little creatures the seeds of all the virtues, all the powers of which they will one day be so much in need; when I perceive in their obstinacy future steadfastness and firmness of character, in their mischievousness good humour and the ease with which they will slide over the perils of the world, and all of it so unspoilt, so complete! – then I repeat over and over again the golden words of the Teacher of men: "Except ye become as little children!"* And now, best of friends, these children, who are like ourselves, whom we should look upon as our models, we treat as subjects. They are not supposed to have a will of their own! Well, don't we have one? On what do we base our prerogative? The fact that we are older and wiser! Good God, from your heaven you see old children and young children, and that is all, and your son proclaimed long ago in which of them you take the greater pleasure. But they believe in him without hearing him – that too is an old story! – and form their children after themselves, and – adieu, Wilhelm! I have no desire to prattle on further.

1st July

I feel in my own poor heart, which is worse off than many a one languishing on a sickbed, what Lotte must mean to a patient. She will spend some days in town at the house of an excellent woman who, the physicians say, is nearing her end, and who wishes to have Lotte near her in these last moments. Last week I went with her to call on the pastor of St ***, a hamlet that lies off to one side in the hills, an hour's walk from here. We got there about four. Lotte had taken her second sister along. When we stepped into the parsonage yard, which is shaded by two tall walnut trees, the good old man was sitting on a bench before the front door, and when he saw Lotte, he was as if rejuvenated, forgot about his stick, and boldly rose to go towards her. She ran up to him and forced him to sit down, seating herself beside him, brought him many greetings from her father, and hugged his odious, filthy youngest boy, the pet of his old age. You should have seen her as she held his full attention, raising her voice to make herself audible to his half-deaf ears, telling him about young, robust persons who had died unexpectedly, about the excellence of Karlsbad, and praised his resolve to go there in the following summer, telling him that he was looking much better, much livelier than the last time she had seen him. Meanwhile I had paid my respects to the pastor's wife. The old man grew quite lively, and since I could not refrain from praising the handsome walnut trees which were shading us so pleasantly, he began, though with some difficulty, to tell us their history.

"As for the old tree," he said, "we don't know who planted it: some say this pastor, some the other. But the younger one back there is as old as my wife, fifty years come October. Her father planted it one morning, and she was born that same day, towards evening. He was my predecessor in office, and there are no words to tell how dear the tree was to him – it is certainly no less dear to me. My wife was sitting under it on a wooden beam, knitting, when I came into this yard as a poor student twenty-seven years ago."

Lotte asked after his daughter and was told that she had gone out with Mr Schmidt to the meadow to talk to the workmen. The old man went on with his story, telling how his predecessor, and the latter's daughter also, had come to like him, and how he had first become his vicar and then his successor. The story had hardly been finished when the pastor's daughter and the aforementioned Mr Schmidt came up through the garden; she welcomed Lotte with heartfelt warmth, and I must say I found her not unpleasing: a sprightly, well-formed brunette, who could have made our short stay in the country quite entertaining. Her lover (for Mr Schmidt promptly presented himself as such), a nice but quiet person, who would not take part in our conversation, although Lotte kept drawing him into it. What distressed me most was that I thought I could read in his features that it was obstinacy and ill humour, rather than a limited intelligence, which prevented him from speaking his mind. Subsequently this became only too plain; for when Friederike during a stroll walked with Lotte, and occasionally with me too, the gentleman's face, which was of a brownish hue to start with, darkened so visibly that it was opportune for Lotte to pluck me by the sleeve and give me to understand that I had been too attentive to Friederike. Now nothing annoys me more than when people torment each other, but most of all when young people in the bloom of life, when they could be supremely open to all joys, spoil the few good days they have together with silly notions, and only too late realize that what they have thrown away is irretrievable. This vexed me, and when we returned to the parsonage towards evening, eating clabber around a table, and the conversation turned upon the joy and sorrow in the world, I could not resist picking up that thread and talking very earnestly against ill humour.

"We often complain," said I, "that there are so few good days, and so many bad ones, and mostly we are wrong, it seems to me. If we always had our hearts open to the enjoyment of the good which God prepares for us day by day, then we would also have strength enough to bear the bad when it comes."

"But we have no control over our feelings," replied the pastor's wife. "How much depends on our body! If we don't feel well, nothing pleases us."

I conceded that. "Let us then," I went on, "regard it as a disease and enquire if there is no remedy for it."

"A good suggestion," said Lotte, "I at least believe that much depends on us. I know that by experience. If something annoys me and tries to make me vexed, I jump up and sing a couple of quadrilles, prancing up and down the garden, and right away it's gone."

"That is what I was going to say," I rejoined: "bad humour is to be treated just like indolence, for it is a kind of indolence. Our nature inclines to it very much, and yet if we once have the force to brace ourselves, the work will go briskly through our hands, and we shall find a true pleasure in being active."

Friederike was very attentive, and the young man raised the objection that one is not master of himself and is least of all able to control his emotions.

"The question here," I replied, "is that of an unpleasant emotion, which surely everyone is glad to be rid of, and no one knows how far his powers will extend until he has tried them out. Certainly, one who is sick will consult all the physicians around, and he will not reject the greatest deprivations or the bitterest drugs in order to regain his cherished good health."

I observed that the honest pastor was straining to hear, so as to take part in our discussion, and I raised my voice as I turned to address him. "They preach against so many vices," I said. "I have never yet heard that anyone has combated ill humour from the pulpit."*

"That would be something for city preachers to do," he said, "peasants have no ill humour. Yet once in a while it would do no harm, it would at least be a lesson to the peasant's wife, and to the Bailiff."

Everyone laughed, and he laughed heartily too, until he fell to coughing, which interrupted our discussion for a while;

thereupon the young fellow resumed: "You called ill humour a vice; that seems to me an exaggeration."

"Not at all," I answered, "if that with which we injure ourselves and our neighbours deserves such a name. Is it not enough that we cannot make each other happy; must we also rob each other of the pleasure that every heart can occasionally give itself? And give me the name of the person who is in an ill humour and at the same time is so noble as to conceal it, to bear it all alone, without spoiling the joy of those around him! Or isn't it rather an inner vexation at our own unworthiness, a displeasure with ourself, always bound up with a hostility egged on by foolish vanity? We see people happy whom *we* are not making so, and that is unendurable."

Lotte smiled at me, seeing the agitation with which I was speaking, and a tear in Friederike's eyes spurred me on to continue. "Woe to those," I said, "who make use of the power they have over another's heart to rob it of the simple joys which are an outgrowth of its own nature. All the gifts, all the little kindnesses in the world will not make up for one moment of enjoyment of oneself which a malice-filled discomfort of our tyrant has embittered."

My whole heart was full at that moment; the recollection of so much that is past pressed in upon my soul, and tears came to my eyes.

"If each one would only say to himself every day," I cried out, "you can have no influence over your friends save by leaving them their joys and increasing their happiness, insofar as you enjoy it with them. If their soul is tortured by a disturbing passion, or distracted by grief, have you the power to give them one drop of balm?

"And then when the last dread disease falls upon the creature that you have undermined in the days of her prime, and now she lies there in a pitiful lassitude, her eyes looking passively heavenwards, the sweat of death shifting on the pale brow, and you stand at her bed like one condemned, feeling to your depths that you can do nothing with all that you own, and fear convulses you inwardly, so that you would like to surrender everything in order to be able to infuse in this perishing creature one drop of invigoration, one spark of courage."

The recollection of such a scene at which I had been present fell upon me at these words with all its force. I put my handkerchief to my eyes and left the room, and only the voice of Lotte, calling to me that we were going to leave, brought me to my senses. And how she scolded me as we went, saying that I took everything too much to heart, and that it would bring me to my death! That I should spare myself! Oh, angel! For your sake I must go on living!

6th July

She is constantly with her dying friend, and she is always the same, always the attentive, lovely creature who, wherever she turns, quiets pain and makes people happy. Yesterday evening she took a walk with Marianne and little Amalia; I knew about it and met them, and we went on together. After a walk of an hour and a half we came back towards the town and reached the spring which has meant so much to me and now means a thousand times more. Lotte sat down on the little coping, we standing before her. I looked about – ah! – and the time when my heart was so alone again came to life for me.

"Dear spring," I said, "of late I have ceased to rest near your coolness, and passing you in haste I have sometimes not even looked at you."

Looking down, I saw Amalia very busily climbing the steps with a glass of water. I looked at Lotte and felt all that she is to me. Meanwhile Amalia came up with the glass. Marianne wanted to take it from her – "No!" cried the child with the sweetest look. "No, Lottie, you must drink first!" I was so enchanted by the sincerity, by the affection of her cry that the only way I had of expressing my emotion was to lift up the child from the ground and kiss her heartily, whereupon she began to weep and wail. "You have done wrong," said Lotte. I was taken aback. "Come, dear," she went on, taking the child by the hand and leading her down the steps, "come and wash yourself with the cool water, quick, quick, then it will be all right." As I stood there and saw with what zeal the little one rubbed her cheeks with her little wet hands, with what faith that the miraculous spring would wash away every impurity and avert the disgrace of growing an ugly beard; as Lotte said, "That's enough," and still the little one kept on eagerly rubbing, as if more would be more effective than little – I tell you, Wilhelm, I have never witnessed a baptism with greater reverence, and when Lotte came up, I would have liked to cast myself down before her as before a prophet who has washed away with holy water the sins of a nation.

That evening I could not refrain, in my heartfelt joy, from relating the incident to a man whom I thought to have human feeling, since he has common sense, but how I put my foot in it! He said that Lotte had done very ill; one should not misinform children; such actions gave rise to countless errors and superstitions, against which one must guard children at an early age. Now it occurred to me that the man had had a child baptized a week before, and so I let it pass, retaining in my heart fidelity to this truth: we should deal with children as God deals with us, for He makes us happiest when He lets us grope our way in a pleasant illusion.

8th July

What children we are! How greedy we are for a certain look! What children we are! We had walked to Wahlheim. The ladies drove out, and during our strolls I thought that in Lotte's black eyes – I am a fool, forgive me! You should see them, those eyes. To make it short (for my eyes are falling shut with sleepiness) – look, the ladies got in, and round the carriage were standing young W., Selstadt and Audran and I. So then there was chat through the carriage door with these lads, who I admit were airy and animated enough. I sought

Lotte's eyes: ah, they were wandering from one to the other!
But on me – me! Me! Who stood there intent upon her alone –
they did not fall! My heart spoke a thousand farewells to her!
And she did not see me! The carriage drove past, and there
was a teardrop in my eye. I looked after her, and saw Lotte's
headdress push out through the door, and she turned to look
– ah! – for me? Friend! This is the uncertainty I am suspended
in; this is my consolation: perhaps she was looking for me!
Perhaps! Good night! Oh what a child I am!

10th July

You should see what a silly figure I cut when she is mentioned
in society! And then if I am even asked how I like her – like!
I hate that word like death. What sort of person must that
be who likes Lotte, in whom all senses, all emotions are not
completely filled up by her! Like! Recently someone asked me
how I like Ossian!

11th July

Mrs M. is in a very bad state; I pray for her life because I suffer
with Lotte. I rarely see her at the house of my lady friend, but
today she told of a marvellous incident. Old M. is a stingy,
niggardly miser, who has roundly tormented and restricted his
wife all her life; yet she always contrived to get along. A few
days ago, when the physician told her she could not live, she
sent for her husband – Lotte was in the room – and addressed
him like this: "I must confess to you a matter which might cause
confusion and vexation after my death. I have kept house all
this time as properly and economically as possible, but you
will forgive me for having deceived you all these thirty years.
At the beginning of our marriage you fixed a small sum for the
expenses of the kitchen and other domestic needs. When our
establishment grew and our business increased, you could not
be induced to increase my weekly allowance in proportion; in

short, you know that in the times when our requirements were at their peak, you demanded that I should get along on seven florins a week. So I took them without demur, and every week I took the rest out of the till, since nobody suspected that a wife would rob the cash box. I didn't waste anything, and I would have confidently faced eternity without this confession, but for the fact that the one who will have to run the house after me would not know what to do, since you could always insist that your first wife had got along on that much."

I discussed with Lotte this incredible self-deception of the human mind: that a man should not suspect some unrevealed explanation when a person gets along on seven florins, although the visible expenditure is perhaps twice that much. But I myself have known people who would have assumed without surprise that their house contained the prophet's never-failing cruse.*

13th July

No, I do not delude myself! I read in her black eyes true sympathy for me, and for my fate. Yes, I feel, and in this I can trust my heart, that she – oh may I, can I utter the heaven that lies in these words? – that she loves me!

Loves me! And how precious I become to myself, how I – I think I may say this to you, for you have understanding for such things – how I adore myself, now that she loves me!

Is this presumptuousness, or a feeling for things as they really are? – I do not know any person whose share in Lotte's heart might cause me apprehension. And yet – when she speaks of her betrothed, speaks of him with such warmth, such love – then I feel like one who is deprived of all his honours and dignities, and whose sword is taken from him.

16th July

Ah, how it courses through my every vein when my finger unexpectedly touches hers, or when our feet encounter

38

each other under the table! I pull back as if singed, and a mysterious force draws me forward again – all my senses reel so. Oh! And her innocence, her unsuspecting soul does not feel how the little intimacies torture me. If in conversation she even lays her hand on mine, and moves closer to me in the interest of the discussion, so that the heavenly breath of her lips can reach mine – I think I am fainting, as if struck by lightning. And, Wilhelm, if I should ever dare to violate this heaven and this confidence!... You know what I mean. No, my heart is not so ruined! It is weak! Weak enough! And doesn't that mean ruin?

She is sacred to me. All physical desire is mute in her presence. I can never tell how I feel when I am with her; it is as if my soul were a whirl in every nerve. There is a melody that she plays on the piano with the touch of an angel, so simple and so full of meaning. It is her favourite tune, and as soon as she plays the first note of it I find myself cured of all grief, bewilderment and cares.

To me nothing that is said about the magic power of ancient music is improbable, seeing how simple singing affects me. And how she has the wit to employ it, often at a time when I should like to put a bullet through my head! Then the darkness and delusion of my soul is dispersed, and again I breathe more freely.

18th July

Wilhelm, of what value to our heart is a world without love? The same as a projector without a light! No sooner have you put in the little lamp than the gayest pictures are shining on your white wall! And even if it were no more than that, mere transient phantoms, still our happiness is in them when we stand before them like unspoilt youngsters, delighting in the wondrous sights. Today I could not go to see Lotte, being detained by an unavoidable engagement. What was to be done? I sent out my servant, merely to have a human being around me who had been near her today. With what impatience I waited for him, with what joy I saw him return! I would have clutched his head and kissed him, if I had not been ashamed to.

They say of Bologna rock that if you lay it in the sun it will draw in the rays and shine for a while at night. So it was with my lad. The feeling that her eyes had rested on his face, his cheeks, his coat buttons, the collar of his overcoat, made all of it so holy to me, so precious! At that moment I would not have given up the lad for a thousand talers. I felt so happy in his presence. God help you if you laugh at this. Wilhelm, when we feel happy, are we seeing phantoms?

19th July

"I shall see her!" I cry in the morning as soon as I am awake, looking towards the beautiful sun with unmixed delight; "I shall see her!" And then for the rest of the day I have no further wish. Everything, everything merges in that one prospect.

20th July

Your idea, yours and Mother's, that I should accompany the ambassador to ***, is not as yet acceptable to me. I am not overly fond of being a subordinate, and besides, we all know that he is an obnoxious person. You said that my mother would like to see me engaged in some activity; that made me laugh. Am I not active as it is? And isn't it basically the same whether I count peas or lentils? Everything in the world comes down to mere trumpery, and a man who wears himself out because others want him to, without gratifying his own passion or satisfying his own needs, but seeking money or prestige, or whatever, is bound to be a fool.

24th July

Since it means so much to you that I should not neglect my sketching, I would rather skip the whole subject than tell you that little is being done all this while.

Never was I happier, never was my feeling for nature more complete and intimate, down to the pebbles, down to the grass blades, and yet – I don't know how to express it, my power of visualization is so feeble, and everything sways and swims so before my soul, that I cannot hold any outline fast; but I have the fancy that if I had clay or wax I could mould it quite well. And if this goes on too long, I *shall* take clay, and knead it, and even if it should turn into a cake!

Three times I have begun a portrait of Lotte, and three times I have made myself ridiculous, which vexes me all the more since I had a very sure hand some time ago. So then I made a silhouette of her, and this must suffice me.

26th July

Yes, dear Lotte, I will take care of and see to everything; just keep on giving me commissions, and do so often. But I have one request of you: strew no more sand on the notes you write me. Today I put it promptly to my lips, and got grit between my teeth.

26th July

I have sometimes resolved not to see her so often. As if a man could stick to that! Every day I succumb to temptation, and then I promise myself solemnly, "Tomorrow for once you will stay away," and when the morning comes, once again I find some irresistible pretext, and before I know it I am with her. Either she has said in the evening, "You're coming tomorrow, aren't you?" And who could stay away after that? Or she gives me some commission, and I find it proper to take the answer to her in person; or the day is just too lovely, I'll go out to Wahlheim, and once I am there, it's only an extra half-hour's walk to her! I am too close to her aura – click! And there I am. My grandmother would tell a tale about the magnet mountain. Ships that came too close were suddenly robbed of all their iron: the nails flew off to the mountain, and the poor wretches drowned, caught in the collapsing hull.

30th July

Albert has come, and I shall go, and even if he were the best and noblest of men, to whom I should be ready to yield in every respect, it would be unendurable to watch him have possession of so many perfections. Possession! Enough, Wilhelm: the betrothed is here! A good and agreeable man whom one cannot but like. Fortunate that I was not present to witness his reception! That would have rent my heart. Yes, and he is so decent that he has not kissed Lotte a single time in my presence. God reward him! I have to love him because of the reverence he shows for the girl. He wishes me well, and I surmise that that is Lotte's doing rather than his own feeling. For in that respect women have a fine instinct, and a sound one: if they can keep two admirers on good terms with each other, that is bound to be to their advantage, however rarely it succeeds.

At the same time I cannot deny Albert my esteem. His outward calm contrasts very vividly with the restlessness of my character, which cannot be concealed. He has deep feeling, and he knows what he has in Lotte. He seems to be rarely in an ill humour, and you know that that is the vice in people which I hate worse than any other.

He regards me as a man of intelligence, and my devotion to Lotte, the warm pleasure I take in all her actions, increases his own triumph and makes him love her all the more. I will leave the question open whether he doesn't sometimes torment her with little jealousies; I at least, were I in his position, would not remain wholly free from such devilry.

Be that as it may. The joy I had in being with Lotte is gone. Shall I call that stupidity or blindness? What need of names? The story tells itself! I knew everything I know now before Albert came; I knew that I had no claims on her, and I made none – that is to say, insofar as it is possible not to desire so lovable an object. And now the simpleton looks on wide-eyed when the other really comes and takes the girl away from him.

I clench my teeth, and mock at my own misery, and would mock twice and thrice over at those who might say that I should resign myself, and that, since it simply can't be otherwise – take these passionless people off my neck! I rove around in the woods, and when I get to Lotte's and Albert is sitting outside with her in the summer house, and I can't do anything else, I lapse into foolish extravagance and begin all sorts of silly and nonsensical talk. "For Heaven's sake," said Lotte to me today, "I beg of you, no such scene as you made last evening! You frighten me when you are so cheerful." Between you and me, I watch for times when he is busy, then whoosh! Out I dash, and I always feel happy if I find her alone.

8th August

I beg you, dear Wilhelm, not to think I was pointing at you when I called unendurable those people who require us to submit to inevitable destiny. Truly, I was not thinking that you too might be of a similar opinion. And basically you are right. Just one thing, however: it is very rare in this world that we can get along with an either-or; feelings and modes of behaviour shade off as diversely as there are gradations between a Roman and a snub nose.

So you will not take it amiss if I concede your whole argument, and still try to squeeze through between your either-or.

Either, you say, you have hopes of Lotte, or you have none. All right, in the first case seek to realize your hope, seek to embrace the fulfilment of your wishes; in the other case, pull yourself together and try to get rid of a wretched emotion which is bound to consume all your powers. My dear fellow! That is well said, and – quickly said.

And can you, if there is a wretch whose life is slowly, irresistibly giving way to a creeping disease, can you demand of him that he should seize a dagger and put a sudden end to his torment? And does not the ailment which is consuming his powers rob him at the same time of the courage to free himself from it?

True, you could answer with a related analogy: who would not rather have his arm cut off than by hesitating and haggling put his life in jeopardy? I don't know! And let us not go on bickering with metaphors. Enough – yes, Wilhelm, sometimes I have a moment of leaping courage and could shake off everything, and then – if I only knew where – I think I would go.

Evening

My diary, which I have been neglecting for some time, got into my hands again today, and I am astonished to see with what awareness I walked into all this, step by step! How I kept a clear picture of my condition, and yet acted like a child, just as right now I see so clearly, and there is no sign of any improvement.

10th August

I could lead the happiest of lives if I were not a fool. It is not often that such favourable circumstances come together to delight the soul of a man as are those in which I find myself at present. Ah, just as certain is it that our heart alone creates its own happiness. To be a member of that lovable family, loved like a son by the father, like a father by the little ones, and by Lotte! Then there is honest Albert, who does not spoil my happiness by any capricious ill temper; who encompasses me with a heartfelt friendship; to whom after Lotte I am the dearest person in the world – Wilhelm, it is a joy to hear us when we go strolling and converse about Lotte: nothing has been discovered in the world more ridiculous than this relationship, and yet it often causes tears to come to my eyes.

When he tells me about her admirable mother: how on her deathbed she entrusted her house and her children to Lotte, and commended Lotte to his care; how since that time a wholly different spirit has animated Lotte; how she, in her concern for the household and in a natural seriousness, has become a true mother; how not a moment of her time has been spent without loving action, without some toil, and yet how her cheerfulness, her sprightly spirit has never forsaken her. I walk along beside him, pick flowers by the wayside, form them very carefully into a bouquet, and – fling them into the passing stream, looking after them as they gently toss their way down. I don't know whether I have written you that Albert will stay here and receive a post, with a very pretty income, from the court, where he is a great favourite. I have seen few to equal him in orderly and zealous dispatch of duties.

12th August

There is no doubt that Albert is the best person in the world. Yesterday I had an extraordinary experience with him. I called on him to take leave of him; for I took a fancy to ride off into the mountains, from where I am just now writing to you, and as I was walking up and down the room, his pistols met my eye. "Lend me the pistols for my trip," said I. "I don't mind," said he, "if you want to take the trouble of loading them; I just hang them up as a matter of form." I took one down, and he continued, "Since my cautiousness once played me such a mean trick, I don't care to have anything more to do with the things." I was curious to hear what had happened. "I lived for a good three months," he said, "in the country house of a friend, had a couple of unloaded pistols and slept undisturbed. One rainy afternoon, as I was sitting idle, the thought came to me, I don't know how: we might be attacked, we might need the pistols and might – well, you know how it is. I gave them to my servant to clean and load, and he dallies with the maids, tries to frighten them and, God knows how, the gun goes off with the ramrod still in it and drives the ramrod into the ball of one girl's right thumb, crushing the thumb. So I had an earful, and had to pay the doctor besides, and since that time I leave all guns unloaded. My dear fellow, what is caution? The forms of danger are infinite! To be sure..." Now you may know that I love this man very much, all but his "to be sure"; for isn't it obvious that every generalization is subject to exceptions? But that's the way this fellow will correct himself! If he thinks he has said something precipitate, too general, half-true, then he never stops limiting, qualifying, adding to it and taking from it, until at last there is nothing left of what he said. And on this occasion he got very deeply involved; finally I stopped listening to him altogether, fell into freakish thoughts, and suddenly leaping up I pressed the mouth of the pistol to my forehead above the right eye. "For shame!" said Albert, pulling the pistol down. "What are you doing?" "It's not loaded," said I. "What if it isn't, why do you do it?" he replied impatiently. "I can't imagine how a person can be so silly as to shoot himself; the mere thought of it repels me."

"Oh that you people," I burst out, "when you mention something, have to say: that is silly, that is wise, that is good, that is bad! And what does it all mean? Has it made you explore the conditions underlying an action? Are you able to unfold with precision the reasons why it happened, why it had to happen? If you had, you wouldn't be so ready with your judgements."

"You will admit," said Albert, "that certain actions remain morally wrong, no matter what their motivations may be."

I shrugged my shoulders and admitted it. "And yet, my good fellow," I went on, "here too there are some exceptions. It is true that theft is a wrong, but does the man who sets out to steal in order to save himself and his family from imminent starvation deserve sympathy or punishment? Who will cast the first stone against the husband who, in righteous wrath, sacrifices his faithless wife and her contemptible seducer? Or against the girl who in an hour of rapture loses self-control in the irresistible joys of love? Even our very laws, cold-blooded pedants that they are, let themselves be moved and withhold their penalties."

"That is an entirely different thing," replied Albert, "because a person who is carried away by his passions loses all power of deliberation and is as good as drunk or mad."

"Oh, you rationalists!" I shouted with a smile. "Passion! Drunkenness! Madness! You stand there so calm, so unsympathetic, you moral men! Chide the drinker, abhor the irrational, walk past like priests, and like the Pharisee thank God that he has not made you like one of these. I have been drunk more than once, my passions were never far from madness, and I repent of neither: for in my own measure I have learnt to understand how it is that all extraordinary beings, who have accomplished something great, something seemingly impossible, have always and necessarily been defamed as drunk and mad.

"But even in ordinary life it is unendurable to hear men exclaim in response to almost any halfway deliberate, noble, unexpected deed: the fellow is drunk, he is crazy! Shame on you sober ones, shame on you sage ones!"

"Here we have some more of your wild ideas," said Albert, "you overdo everything, and in this case you are at least wrong in comparing suicide, which was our last topic, with great actions: since it can certainly not be regarded as anything but a weakness. For it is admittedly easier to die than to endure a life of torment with steadfastness."

I was on the point of breaking off; for no argument robs me so of composure as when a man comes along with an insignificant commonplace when I am expressing the depths of my heart.

But I composed myself, because I had often heard that, and had often been vexed by it, and retorted with some vivacity, "You call that weakness? I beg you not to let yourself be misled by appearances. If a nation is sighing under the unendurable yoke of a tyrant, do you dare speak of weakness if the people rise up in rage and rend their fetters? If a man, gripped by the terror of having his house seized by fire, feels all his strength heightened and carries off with ease burdens which he can scarcely move when his mind is calm; if another, furious with outrage, stands up against six others and overpowers them – are they to be called weak? And, my good fellow, if exertion is strength, why should overexertion be the opposite?"

Albert looked at me and said, "Don't take it amiss, but the examples you cite don't seem to be pertinent here." "That may be," said I. "I have often been told that my way of combining things sometimes borders on absurdity. Let us see, then, whether we can imagine in some other way how a man must feel who resolves to cast off the otherwise agreeable load of life. For only insofar as we have fellow feelings are we entitled to discuss such a matter.

"Human nature," I continued, "has its bounds: it can endure joy, sorrow, pain, up to a certain degree, and it perishes as soon as that degree is exceeded. In this case it is then not a question of whether a man is weak or strong, but whether he can outlast the measure of his suffering – be it spiritual or physical – and I find it just as strange to say that the man who takes his life is a coward, as it would be improper to call a man cowardly who dies of a malignant fever."

"Paradoxical! Most paradoxical!" cried Albert.

"Not as much as you think," I replied. "You will admit that we call it a mortal sickness when a body is so assailed that in part its forces are consumed, in part robbed of effectiveness, that it is no longer capable of restoring itself, or of resuming, by any fortunate turn of things, the customary course of life.

"Now then, my friend, let us apply this to the mind. Behold the human being in his confined state and see how impressions affect him, take a firm hold on him, until at last a growing passion robs him of all calm power of thought and drives him to destruction.

"In vain does a calm, rational person diagnose the unhappy man's condition, in vain does he try to give him courage! Just as a healthy man who stands at the bedside of a sick one cannot infuse into him the least bit of his own strength."

For Albert this exposition was too general. I reminded him of a girl that had recently been found dead in the water, and repeated her story to him. A young, good creature who had grown up in the narrow round of domestic occupations, definite weekly chores, who had no other prospect of pleasure than perhaps to go strolling about the town with her companions on a Sunday, in finery that she had acquired little by little, perhaps to go dancing when the chief holidays came around, and for the rest to spend an occasional hour, with all the vivacity of sincere interest, in chatting with a neighbour woman about some quarrel, some bit of evil gossip – whose ardent nature at last feels some more tender needs, which are increased by the flatteries of men. Her previous pleasures gradually lose their savour for her, until finally she meets a man to whom she is irresistibly drawn by an unfamiliar emotion, on whom she pins all her hopes, forgetting the world around her, and hears nothing, sees nothing, feels nothing but him, the only one, yearns only for him, the only one. Not spoilt by the empty diversions of an inconstant vanity, her desire goes straight to the point: she wants to become his, to find in a lasting union all the happiness that she lacks, to taste in one concentration all the joys for which she has longed. Repeated promises that put the seal on the certainty of all her hopes, bold caresses which heighten her desires, encompass her whole soul; she is afloat in a vague awareness, in a foretaste of all joys, her tension attains the highest peak, at last she stretches out her arms to embrace all she has wished for – and her beloved forsakes her. Paralysed, without sensation, she sees herself before an abyss; all is darkness about her, no prospects, no consolation, no hope! For *he* has forsaken her in whom alone she felt her existence to be. She does not see the wide world that lies before her, nor the many souls who might make up for her loss; she feels herself alone, forsaken by everyone – and blindly, driven into a corner by the fearful affliction of her heart, she flings herself down, to stifle all her torments in one all-embracing death. Look, Albert, that is the story of so many a human being! And tell me, is that not the same as a disease? Nature finds no way out of the labyrinth of tangled and contradictory forces, and the human being has to die.

"Woe to him who could look on and say, 'Foolish girl! Had she waited, had she let time have its effect, despair would surely have abated, and surely someone else would have come forward to comfort her.' Just as if one should say, 'What a fool to die of fever! Had he waited until his powers had recovered, his life forces improved, the tumult of his blood abated, then all would have gone well, and he would be alive today!'"

Albert, who still could not visualize this comparison, made some objections, including this one: I had spoken only of a simple-minded girl, but he could not comprehend how a man of reason, who was not so limited, who had a broader grasp on things, could be excusable. "My friend," I cried, "human beings are human, and the bit of common sense a man may have counts for little or nothing when passions rage and the bounds of humanness press in on us. Say rather – we'll come back to this," said I, reaching for my hat. Oh, my heart was so full – and we parted without having understood each other. As indeed it is not easy in this world for one person to understand the next one.

15th August

It is surely a fact that nothing in the world but love makes a person indispensable. Lotte makes me feel that she would dislike to lose me, and the children have no other idea but that I would keep coming morning after morning. Today I had gone out to tune Lotte's piano, but I couldn't get to it, for the little ones pursued me with a request for a fairy tale, and Lotte herself said that I should give them their way. I cut the bread for their supper – they now take it from me almost as willingly as from Lotte – and told them the capital tale about the princess who is served by hands. I learn much in doing so, I assure you, and I am astonished at the impression it makes on them. Because I sometimes have to invent a detail that I forget the next time, they say right away that last time it was different, so that I am now training myself to recite them unalterably in a sing-song and as straight as a string. I have learnt from this that an author must necessarily injure his book by issuing a second revised edition of his story, even though it should be poetically ever so much improved. The first impression finds us willing listeners, and man is so made that one can persuade him of the most fantastic happenings, but they also stick fast in his memory, and woe to him who tries to erase and obliterate them again!

18th August

Was it necessary, I wonder, that that which makes the happiness of a man should also become the source of his misery?

The warm, rich feeling of my heart for living nature, which flooded me with so much rapture, which turned the world around me into a paradise, is now becoming an unendurable tormentor to me, a torturing spirit that pursues me on all my ways. Whereas formerly I would survey the fruitful valley from the cliffs, looking across the river towards yonder heights, and seeing everything around me sprouting and swelling; whereas I saw those mountains, from the foot all the way to the summit, clad with a dense growth of tall trees, and those valleys in their manifold windings shaded by the loveliest groves, while the gentle stream flowed along among the whispering reeds and mirrored the beloved clouds that the light breeze wafted across the evening sky; and then I would hear the birds around me bring the woods to life, and the millions of swarming mites danced bravely in the last red rays of the sun, whose last quivering glance freed the buzzing beetle from its grass, and the humming and stirring about me drew my attention to the earth, and the moss, which wrests its nourishment from my resistant rocks, and the underbrush that creeps down the sandy slope would reveal to me the glowing inner holy life of nature – how I would take all that into my warm heart, feeling myself as it were deified in the overflowing abundance, and all the glorious forms of this infinite world come to life within my soul. Monstrous mountains invested me, abysses lay before me, and mountain torrents plunged downwards, the rivers flowed below me, and woods and wilds resounded; and I saw all the unfathomable forces in the depths of the earth working and creating within each other; and now above the ground and under the sky swarm the living creatures in their untold diversity. Everything, everything peopled with myriads of forms, and then the people seeking joint security in their little houses, and building their nests, and ruling in their minds over the wide world! Poor fool that you are! Deeming everything so insignificant because *you* are so small. From the inaccessible mountains across the desert that no foot has trodden, and on to the end of the unknown ocean, breathes the spirit of the eternally creating One, rejoicing in every speck of dust that hears Him and is alive. Ah, in those days, how often did my longing take the wings of a crane that flew overhead and carry me to the shore of the uncharted sea, to drink from the foaming cup of the infinite that swelling rapture of life, and to taste but for an instant, despite the limited force of my soul, one drop of the bliss of that being which produces all things in and by means of itself.

My brother, the mere recollection of those hours does me good. Even this present effort to recall those unspeakable feelings, to utter them again, lifts my soul out of itself, and then makes me feel doubly the anxiety of the state which surrounds me now.

It is as if a curtain had pulled aside before my soul, and the stage of infinite life is transforming itself before me into the abyss of an eternally open grave. Can you say, "This is!" when everything is transitory? When everything rolls by with lightning speed and so seldom expands the entire potential of its existence – ah! – is swept away in the stream, sucked under, and dashed to bits on the rocks? There is no moment which does not consume you and yours with you, no moment when you are not – and of necessity – a destroyer; the most innocent stroll costs a thousand crawlers their life, as *one* step destroys the laborious structures of the ants, trampling a little world into an ignominious grave. Ha! It is not the great, rare catastrophes in the world, the floods that wash away your villages, the earthquakes that engulf your cities, which touch me; what undermines my heart is the consuming power which lies hidden in the whole of nature; power which has formed nothing that does not destroy its neighbour, destroy its own self. And so I stagger on in terror! Heaven and earth and their interplaying forces all around me! I see nothing but a monster which, eternally swallowing, chews its eternal cud.

21st August

In vain I stretch out my arms towards her, in the mornings, when I rouse vaguely from bad dreams, in vain I seek her by night in my bed, when some happy, harmless dream has deluded me into thinking that I was sitting beside her on the meadow, holding her hand and covering it with a thousand kisses. Ah, then when I grope for her, still half-drugged with sleep, and thus wake myself up – a flood of tears bursts from my straining heart, and I weep disconsolate towards a gloomy future.

22nd August

It is a misfortune, Wilhelm: my active powers are dulled into a restless lassitude, and I cannot be idle, and yet I cannot do anything either. I have no power of imagination, no feeling for nature, and books disgust me. If we lose ourselves, we lose everything else too. I swear to you, sometimes I would wish to be a day labourer, merely to have on awaking in the morning a prospect for the day to come, an urge, a hope. Often I envy Albert, whom I see buried in documents up to his ears, and I imagine that I would be happy if I were in his place. Several times before this I have suddenly taken the notion of writing to you and to the minister of state, to apply for that position in the embassy which, as you assure me, would not be refused me. I believe that. The minister has liked me for a long time, and has long been urging me to devote myself to some fixed occupation, and for an hour I may feel like doing so. Later, when I think of it again, and I recall the fable of the horse which, dissatisfied with its freedom, has saddle and bridle put on it and is ridden half to death* – I don't know what I should do. And listen! Isn't the longing in me for a change of state perhaps an uncomfortable impatience of soul which will pursue me everywhere?

28th August

It is true that if my sickness could be cured, these people would cure it. Today is my birthday,* and the first thing in the morning I receive a little package from Albert. On opening it I immediately catch sight of one of the pale-pink bows which Lotte was wearing when I made her acquaintance, and for which I have asked her several times since then. There were two booklets in duodecimo with it, the little Wetstein edition of Homer, one which I have so often wanted, so as not to have to carry the big Ernesti edition when I went walking. Look! Thus they anticipate my wishes, go looking for all the little favours of friendship, which mean a thousand times more than those ostentatious gifts whereby the giver's vanity humiliates us. I kiss this bow a thousand times over, and with every breath I sip the recollection of the raptures with which those few happy, irretrievable days filled me to overflowing. Wilhelm, it is a fact, and I do not grumble at it: life's flowers are mere apparitions! How many of them fade away without leaving a trace, how few of them set as fruit, and how few of those fruits ripen! And yet there are still enough of them on hand; and yet – O, my brother! – can we see such ripened fruits and neglect or despise them, let them decay untasted?

Farewell! It is glorious summer weather, and I often sit in the fruit trees in Lotte's orchard with the fruit-picker, that long pole, and pull down the pears from the treetop. She stands below and takes them when I lower them to her.

30th August

Unhappy man! Are you not a fool? Aren't you deceiving yourself? What avails this raging, endless passion? I have no more prayers to say except to her; my imagination perceives no other figure than hers, and I see everything in the world around me merely in relation to her. And that does give me many a happy hour – until I again have to tear myself away from her! Ah, Wilhelm! What my heart often urges upon me! When I have sat beside her, two hours, or three, and have feasted myself on her figure, on her behaviour, on the divine expression of her sayings, and little by little all my senses come under tension, and it grows dark before my eyes, and I scarcely hear anything, and it clutches at my throat like the hand of an assassin, and then my heart tries to relieve my straining senses by its wild throbbing and only increases their distraction – Wilhelm, I often don't know whether I am on the earth! And – if sorrow does not gain the upper hand, occasionally, so that Lotte allows me the wretched consolation of weeping out my anguish upon her hand – then I have to leave, go far off! And then I rove far afield; then it is joy to me to climb a steep mountain, to work my way through a pathless forest, through hedges that wound me, through brambles that tear my flesh! Then I begin to feel somewhat better! Somewhat! And if I sometimes lie still en route because of exhaustion and thirst, or sometimes, in the dead of night when the full moon hangs high above me, in a lonesome wood, seat myself on a gnarled tree, merely to give some relief to my sore feet, and then doze off in a sleep of exhaustion in that dim radiance! O Wilhelm! Solitary housing in a hermit's cell, a haircloth garment and a belt of thorns, would be restoratives for which my soul is languishing. Adieu! I see no end to this misery save the grave.

3rd September

I must go! I thank you, Wilhelm, for having confirmed my wavering resolve. For two weeks now I have been thinking of leaving her. I must go. She is in town again at the house of a friend. And Albert – and – I must go!

10th September

That was a night! Wilhelm! Now I can survive anything. I shall not see her again! Oh that I cannot rush to fall on your neck, cannot express to you, best friend, amid a thousand tears and transports, the emotions that are assailing my heart. Here I sit and gasp for air, try to calm myself, and await the morning, and the horses are ordered for sunrise.

Ah, she is sleeping peacefully and does not know that she will never see me again. I tore myself away, and was strong enough not to betray my intention in a conversation lasting two hours. And good Heavens, what a conversation!

Albert had promised me that he would be in the garden with Lotte after supper. I stood on the terrace under the tall chestnut trees and looked after the sun as it set, for the last time for me, over the lovely valley, over the gentle stream. So often I had stood there with her and watched that same glorious spectacle, and now – I walked up and down the avenue that was so dear to me; a secret bond of sympathy had so often held me here, even before I knew Lotte, and how glad we were when we discovered, at the beginning of our acquaintance, our mutual affection for this spot, which is in truth one of the most romantic that I have ever seen portrayed by an artist.

First you have, between the chestnut trees, the extensive view – oh, I remember, I think I have already written you much about it, how tall walls of beech finally invest one, and how an adjacent grove makes the avenue more and more dark, until at last everything ends in a small, enclosed spot around which all the tremors of solitude seem to float. I can still feel how homelike it seemed when I stepped into it for the first time at high noon; I had a faint premonition of what a stage that was to become for bliss and bane.

I had basked for perhaps a half-hour in the languishingly sweet thoughts of departure and of return, when I heard them mounting the terrace. I ran towards them, and with a shiver I seized her hand and kissed it. We had just reached the top when the moon rose behind the shrubs on the hill; we talked about various things and approached unawares the dark arbour. Lotte went in and sat down, Albert at her side, and I too, but my unrest would not let me sit long; I got up, stepped in front of her, paced back and forth, sat down again: it was a disquieting situation. She called our attention to the beautiful effect of the moonlight, which was illuminating the entire terrace before us at the end of the walls of beech: a glorious sight, which was all the more striking since we were invested all around by pronounced twilight. We were silent, and after a while she began, "I never go walking in the moonlight, never, without encountering the thought of my departed ones, without having the feeling of death and of the future come over me. We shall live!" she continued in a voice of the most glorious feeling. "But, Werther, shall we find each other again? know each other again? What is your premonition? What do you say?"

"Lotte," said I, as I held out my hand to her and my eyes filled with tears, "we shall see each other again! Here again and there again!" I could not say more – Wilhelm, did she have to ask me that when I had this fearful parting on my mind?

"And I wonder if the dear departed know about us," she went on, "if they feel, when we are well off, that we recall them with warm affection. Oh! The form of my mother always hovers about me when I sit of a quiet evening among her children, among my children, and they are gathered about me as they used to be gathered about her. Then when I look heavenwards with a yearning tear, and wish that she might look in for a moment to see how I am keeping my word, that I gave her in the hour of her death: to be the mother of her children. With what emotion I exclaim, 'Forgive me, dearest mother, if I am not what you were to them. Ah! Surely I do all that I can; surely they are dressed, nourished, yes, and what is more than all else, cared for and loved. Could you see our harmony, dear saint! You would glorify with the most fervent thanks the God Whom you besought with your last and bitterest tears for the welfare of your children.'"

So she spoke! O Wilhelm, who can repeat what she said? How can cold, lifeless letters represent this glorious flower of the spirit? Albert interrupted her gently: "This is too hard on you,* dear Lotte! I know that your soul inclines much to these ideas, but I beg you—"

"O Albert," said she, "I know that you have not forgotten the evenings when we would sit together at the little round table when Papa was away and we had put the little ones to bed. You often had a good book, and so rarely found time to read anything – was not our intercourse with that wonderful soul more than all else? That beautiful, gentle, cheerful and always active woman! God knows about the tears with which I often cast myself before Him in my bed, praying that He would make me like her."

"Lotte," I cried, as I cast myself down before her, took her hand and moistened it with a thousand tears, "Lotte, the blessing of God rests upon you, and the spirit of your mother!"

"If you had known her," she said, as she pressed my hand, "she was worthy of your acquaintance!" I thought I would swoon. Never had a greater, prouder thing been uttered about me – and she continued, "And this woman had to go in the prime of her life, when her youngest son was not six months old! Her sickness did not last long; she was calm, resigned, and only the thought of her children caused her grief, especially the baby. When the end neared, and she said to me, 'Bring them up here,' and I led them in, the little ones knowing nothing, and the older ones beside themselves as they stood around the bed, and how she lifted her hands and prayed over them, and kissed one after the other and sent them away, and said to me, 'Be a mother to them!' – I gave her my hand on it! – 'You are promising much, my daughter,' said she, 'the heart of a mother and the eyes of a mother. I have often seen by your grateful tears that you feel what that is. Have that for your siblings, and have for your father the loyalty and the obedience of a wife. You will console him.' She asked for him, but he had gone out to spare us the unbearable grief he was feeling, for the man's heart was rent.

"Albert, you were in the room. She heard someone's footsteps and enquired, and had you come to her, and when she looked at you and me, with the calm and comforted gaze that knew we would be happy, happy together—" Albert flung his arms around her and kissed her and cried, "We are happy! We shall be!" Our quiet Albert was quite beside himself, and I had forgotten who I was.

"Werther," she recommenced, "to think that this woman should be gone! Heavens! Sometimes I think how we let the dearest thing in life be borne away, and how no one but the children feel that so keenly, the children who kept complaining that the black men had carried off their mama."

She got up, and I, restored to reality and shaken, remained sitting and held her hand. "Let us go," said she, "it is time now." She tried to withdraw her hand, and I held it more tightly. "We shall see each other again," I cried, "we shall find each other, we shall recognize each other amid all the figures there are. I am going," I continued, "going willingly, and yet, if I were to say 'for ever', I should not endure it. Farewell, Lotte! Farewell, Albert! We shall meet again."

"Tomorrow, I imagine," she replied in jest. I felt that "Tomorrow!" Ah, she did not know, as she drew her hand out of mine. They walked out through the avenue, and I stood and looked after them in the moonlight, and flung myself on the ground and cried myself out, and leapt up, and ran out onto the terrace in time to see her white dress shimmering towards the garden gate, down yonder in the shade of the tall lindens: I stretched out my arms and it vanished.

Second Book

20th October 1771

We arrived here yesterday. The Ambassador is not well, and so he will stay in for some days. If only he were not so ungracious, all would be well. I see, I see, Fate has assigned severe tests to me. But courage! A light heart endures everything! A light heart? It makes me laugh that that word gets into my pen. Oh, a little lighter blood would make me the happiest man under the sun. What! When others are strutting around here in my presence in complacent self-satisfaction with their bit of talent and ability, I should despair of my ability, of my gifts? You, good God, who gave me all this, why did you not withhold the half of it and make me self-confident and contented?

Patience, patience! Things will improve. For I tell you, Wilhelm, you are right. Now that I am pushed around among these people every day, and see what they do and how they do it, I am in much greater favour with myself. It is certain that since we are so made as to compare everyone with ourselves and ourselves with everyone, happiness or misery lies in those circumstances with which we associate ourselves, and then nothing is more dangerous than solitude. Our imagination, impelled by nature to assert itself, nourished by the fantastic images of the poet's art, invents a hierarchy of being of which we are the lowest, while everyone else appears more splendid, more perfect. And that is a wholly natural affair. So often we feel that much is lacking in us, and another often seems to possess just that which we lack, to whom we then ascribe all that we do have, and a certain ideal degree of contentment besides. And thus the happy man stands there complete, our own creation.

If on the other hand we just keep working straight ahead, with all our weakness and strain, we very often find that we get further with our tacking and tardiness than others with their sailing and rowing – and surely one has a true feeling of one's worth when one keeps pace with others or even outruns them.

26th November

I am beginning to feel quite at ease here, considering. The best of it is that there is enough to do, and then the various kinds of people, all sorts of new figures, present a motley spectacle to my soul. I have made the acquaintance of Count C., a man for whom I feel a greater veneration every day, a great and capacious mind, and one who is not cold because of his broad knowledge, whose conversation radiates so much feeling for friendship and love. He took an interest in me when I carried out a commission that took me to him and he observed at our first words that we understood each other, and that he could talk with me as he could not with everyone. Also, I cannot praise too highly his frank behaviour towards me. There is no such true, warm pleasure in the world as to see a great soul which opens up to us.

24th December

The Ambassador causes me much vexation, as I foresaw. He is the most punctilious fool that can exist: one step at a time and as fussy as an old woman; a person who is never content with himself, and whom consequently no one else can satisfy. I like to work straight ahead, and let it stand as it stands, but he is capable of handing a report back to me and saying, "It is good, but look it over: one can always find a better word, a neater particle." That makes me wild. No "and", no connective may be left out, and he is a mortal foe of all inversions, which I sometimes let slip; if you don't drone out your periods according to the traditional melody, he doesn't understand a word. It is a pain to have to do with such a person.

The confidence of Count C. is as yet the only thing that makes up for it. Lately he told me quite frankly how dissatisfied he is with the slowness and inanity of my ambassador. "Such people make things hard for themselves and others; yet," said he, "one must resign oneself to that, like a traveller who has to cross over a mountain: to be sure, if the mountain were not there, the way would be much easier and shorter; but it *is* there, and it must be crossed!"

I think that my chief also detects the preference that the Count gives me over him, and that annoys him, and he takes every opportunity to talk ill of the Count to me; I naturally take the opposite side, and that only makes the matter worse. Yesterday he really aroused me, for I was involved too: he said the Count was quite good at general affairs, for he could work quickly and wrote in a good style, but he was lacking in thorough scholarship, like all literary folk. He wore an expression that seemed to say, "Do you feel the stab?" But it failed to affect me; I despised a man who could think and behave like that. I stood my ground and fought back with considerable vehemence. I said the Count was a man for whom one must feel respect, on account of his character as well as his knowledge. "I have not known anyone," I said, "who has succeeded so well in enlarging his mind so as to cover countless subjects, while continuing to be active in public affairs." This was all Greek to his mind, and I took my leave to avoid swallowing more gall in response to some further twaddle.

And for this all you are to blame who talked me into taking this yoke upon myself, and prated so much about activity. Activity! If a man who plants potatoes or rides into town to sell his corn doesn't do more than I, then I will spend ten years wearing myself out in the galley to which I am now chained.

And the resplendent misery, the boredom among the repulsive crowd that finds itself thrown together here! The petty rivalry among them, as they just watch and wait to get one single step ahead of each other; the wretchedest, most pitiful passions, quite unmasked. There is a woman, for example, who converses with everyone about her rank and her country, so that every stranger must think, "This is a foolish woman who puts on great airs concerning her bit of noble blood and the prestige of her nation." But it is even much worse: this very woman was born right here in the vicinity as the daughter of a secretarial clerk. Look, I can't understand the human race, when it has so little sense as to make such a downright fool of itself.

To be sure, I observe more clearly every day, my friend, how silly we are to judge others by ourselves. And because I am so much concerned with myself, and because this heart is so tempestuous – ah, I am glad to let the others go their way, if only they could let me go mine.

What piques me most is the odious social distinctions. Now I know as well as the next man how necessary differences in rank are, how many advantages they give even to me; but they shouldn't get in my way just when I might enjoy a little pleasure, a gleam of happiness on this earth. While out walking lately I got to know a Miss von B., an agreeable person, who has preserved much naturalness in the midst of this formal existence. We took pleasure in conversing, and as we parted I asked for permission to call on her. She granted it with so much ingenuousness that I could hardly wait for a suitable moment to call. This is not her home, and she is living in an aunt's house. The old lady's physiognomy did not please me. I was very attentive to her, I addressed myself mostly to her, and in less than half an hour I had pretty well guessed what the girl herself confessed later on: that her beloved aunt has a lack of everything in her old age, has no decent income, no intellect, and no support except the long line of her forebears, no protection but the rank which she employs like a barricade, and no pleasure except that of looking down from her top storey upon the heads of the common citizens. In her youth she is said to have been beautiful and to have frittered away her life, first tormenting many a poor youth with her capriciousness, and in maturer years submitting to the tyranny of an old officer, who in return for this price and a tolerable living spent her bronze age* with her, and died. Now she finds herself alone in her iron age, and no one would look at her if her niece were not so lovable.

8th January 1772

What sort of people are they whose whole soul is wrapped up in ceremony, whose entire striving and contriving is devoted to the goal of moving their chair one place nearer the head of the table? And it isn't as if they had nothing else to do: no, on the contrary, the work piles up, just because the little vexations keep people from taking care of the important matters. Last week there was a quarrel during the sleighing party, and all the fun was spoilt.

How foolish not to see that the place you occupy really makes no difference, and that the one who occupies the first place so seldom plays the first role! How many kings are ruled by their ministers, how many ministers by their secretaries! And then who is first? It is he, I think, who surveys the rest, and who has so much power or cunning as to harness their abilities and passions to the execution of his plans.

20th January

I must write you, dear Lotte, here in the good room of a poor peasant inn, in which I have taken refuge from a hard storm. As long as I moved about that sad hole of a town, D., amid alien people, wholly alien to my heart, I never had a moment, not one, in which my heart bade me write to you, and now in this humble hut, in this solitude, in this confinement, while snow and hail are pounding furiously on my little window, here my first thought was of you. As I stepped in, upon me descended your figure, your memory, O Lotte! So sacred, so warm! Kindly God! The first happy moment in all this time.

If you saw me, best of women, in this surge of distractions! And saw how desiccated my senses become; not *one* moment of heartfelt being, not *one* hour of bliss! Nothing! Nothing! I stand as before a raree show, and watch the manikins and tiny horses move about, and often ask myself whether it is not an optical illusion. I play too, or rather, I am played with, like a marionette, and sometimes I seize my neighbour by his wooden hand and draw back shuddering. Of an evening I will resolve to enjoy the sunrise, and yet I don't quit my bed; by day I hope to be gladdened by the moonlight, and yet I stay in my room. I don't rightly know why I get up, why I go to bed.

The leaven which set my life in motion is lacking; the stimulus which kept me awake in the dark of night is gone, and that which woke me from sleep in the morning is no more.

There is only one female creature whom I have met here, a Miss von B., who resembles you, dear Lotte, if it is possible to resemble you. "Well," you will say, "this fellow is going in for pretty compliments!" Not altogether false. For some time I have been very gallant, because I can't be otherwise. I display much wit, and the ladies say that no one manages to utter praise as finely as I (and lies, you will add, for that is an essential part of it, you understand?). But I was going to speak of Miss B. She has a great soul, which is plainly visible in the gaze of her blue eyes. Her rank is burdensome to her, satisfying none of the desires of her heart. She longs to escape from this turmoil, and we spend many an hour in imagining ourselves in rural scenes of unmixed happiness – ah! – and in your company! How often she has to pay homage to you: no, she doesn't have to, she does so voluntarily, likes so much to hear things about you, loves you.

Oh, I wish I were sitting at your feet in the dear, familiar little room, with our little treasures playfully tumbling all around me, and if they grew too noisy for you, I would gather them about me and silence them with some hair-raising tale.

The sun is setting in glory over the land with its glittering snow, the storm has passed by, and I – must lock myself up in my cage again – Adieu! Is Albert with you? And how – ? God forgive me that question!

8th February

For a week we have been having the most abominable weather, and to me that is a benefit. For during all the time I have been here not a single fine day has shown itself to me in the sky that someone has not spoilt or embittered for me. So when it rains very hard, or drizzles, or freezes, or thaws – ah ha! I think it can't be any worse in the house than it is outside, or vice versa, and then I'm content. If the sun at rising in the morning gives promise of a fine day, I can never help crying out: there again they have a divine gift of which they can deprive each other. There is nothing of which they don't deprive each other. Health, good repute, joyousness, recreation! And mostly because of silliness, lack of sense and narrow-mindedness, and, if they are to be believed, with the best intentions. Sometimes I should like to beg them on my knees not to attack their own insides so furiously.

17th February

I fear that my ambassador and I will not endure each other's company much longer. The man is utterly unbearable. His manner of working and doing business is so ridiculous that I cannot refrain from opposing him and frequently doing something according to my ideas and my system, which, naturally enough, never suits him. In this regard he lately complained of me at court, and the minister gave me a rebuke which was, to be sure, gentle, but a rebuke for all that, and I was on the point of requesting my dismissal, when I received from him a private letter,* one before which I fell on my knees, paying homage to that lofty, wise and noble mind. How he reproves my excessive sensitiveness, how he respects, to be sure, as good and youthful spirit, my extreme notions of effective work, of influencing others, of carrying affairs to success, and does not attempt to extirpate them, merely to mitigate and lead them into channels where they will have their proper play and can have the most powerful effect. So I too am strengthened for another week, and again at one with myself. Calmness of soul is a glorious thing, and contentment with oneself. Ah, my friend, if only that jewel were not just as frail as it is precious and beautiful.

20th February

God bless you, my dear ones, and give you all the good days He subtracts from mine!

I thank you, Albert, for having deceived me: I was waiting to hear when your wedding day was to be, and I had resolved to remove Lotte's silhouette solemnly from the wall on that day, and to bury it among other papers. And now you are a pair, and her image is still here! Well, then let it remain so! And why not? I know that I am with you too, that I am, without injury to you, in Lotte's heart, and have, yes, have the second place in it, and I will and must keep that. Oh I should go mad if she could forget – Albert, all hell lies in that thought. Albert, farewell! Farewell, angel of heaven! Farewell, Lotte!

15th March

I have suffered a vexation which will drive me away from here. I am grinding my teeth! Devils! It is not to be made good, and at bottom you are to blame for it, you who goaded and drove and tormented me to put myself into a position which was not to my liking. And now I have it! And you have it! And to keep you from saying once more that my extravagant notions ruined everything, here you have an account, my dear sir, neat and plain, such as a chronicler would set down.

Count von C. loves me, singles me out; this is well known, and I have told you so a hundred times. Now I was at dinner yesterday at his house, and it was the very day when the aristocratic company of lords and ladies assemble there, a fact which I did not remember, nor did it occur to me that we inferior beings have no right to be in it. Good, I dine with the Count, and after dinner we walk up and down in the great hall, I talking with him and with Colonel B., who joins us, and so the hour for the assembly approaches. God knows, I don't give it a thought. In walks my super-snobbish Lady von S. with her noble consort, and her nobly hatched goose of a daughter with the flat breast and the dainty bodice, and in passing they widen their nostrils and stare with traditionally aristocratic eyes, and since that tribe is heartily distasteful to me, I was just going to take my leave, and was only waiting until the Count should be free of that dreadful twaddle, when my Miss B. comes in. As I always feel a little lifting of the heart when I see her, I remained, placed myself behind her chair, and only observed after some time that she was talking to me with less candour than usual, with some embarrassment. I was struck by this. Is she too like all these others? I thought, and was hurt and wanted to leave, and yet I stayed, because I would have liked to find an excuse for her, and was incredulous, and was hoping for another kind word from her and – what you will. Meantime the company was filling up. Baron F., with his entire wardrobe from the days of the coronation of Francis I, Councillor R., designated here, however, *in qualitate* as von R., with his deaf wife, etc., not forgetting the poorly equipped J., who fills up the gaps in his antiquated garb with newfangled trappings – such folk come in droves, and I speak with a few acquaintances, all of whom are very laconic, I thought – and paid heed to no one but my B. I did not observe that the women at the end of the hall were whispering into each other's ears, that it was percolating to the men, that Lady von S. was talking to the Count (Miss B.

told me all this afterwards), until at last the Count walked up to me and drew me over to a window. "You know," said he, "our quaint ways: the company is displeased, I observe, at seeing you here; I would not for the world—"

"Your Excellency," I broke in, "I beg a thousand pardons; I should have thought of this sooner, and I am sure you will forgive me this forgetfulness. I was going to take my leave some time ago, but some evil spirit held me back," I added with a smile, bowing. The Count pressed my hands with a warmth of feeling that was unmistakable. I stole quietly out of the aristocratic gathering, went out, got into a cabriolet and drove to M. to watch the sunset from the height there, reading at the same time in my Homer the fine canto in which Ulysses enjoys the hospitality of the excellent swineherd. All that was good.

In the evening I came back to dinner, there being but few in the dining room; they were playing dice on a corner of the table, with the cloth turned back. Now honest Adelin comes in, lays down his hat on seeing me, comes up to me, and says softly, "You suffered a vexation?"

"I?" said I.

"The Count expelled you from the company."

"To the devil with them!" I said. "I was glad to get out into the fresh air."

"It's good," said he, "that you take it so lightly; only it does vex me, for everyone is talking about it." Now for the first time the affair began to annoy me. All who came to dinner and looked at me made me think, "That is why they are looking at you." That created a bad feeling.

But worse than that, when I am pitied today wherever I show up, when I hear that my rivals are triumphing and saying that this just shows what happens to the upstarts whose bit of intelligence makes them conceited, so that they think they have a right to override all the social conventions, and all the rest of the vile gossip – you feel like sticking a knife into your heart; for whatever may be said about being independent, I'd like to see the man who can endure to let the rascals talk against him when they have an advantage over him; if their talk is baseless, yes, then it's easy to ignore them.

16th March

Everything is harassing me. Today I met Miss B. in the avenue, and could not refrain from speaking to her, and, as soon as we were somewhat separated from the rest, revealing my hurt at her recent behaviour. "O Werther," she said with a sincere tone, "could you so interpret my confusion, you who know my heart? What I suffered on your account, from the moment when I entered the hall! I foresaw everything, and a hundred times it was on my tongue to tell you. I knew that Lady von S. and Lady von T. would sooner leave with their husbands than remain in your company! I knew that the Count must not spoil his friendship with you – and now all this to-do!"

"How so, dear lady?" I said, concealing my alarm; for all that Adelin had said to me the day before yesterday ran at that moment through my veins like boiling water.

"How much it has cost me up to now!" said the sweet creature, with tears in her eyes. I was no longer master of myself, and was on the point of casting myself at her feet. "Explain yourself," I cried. The tears ran down her cheeks. I was beside myself. She wiped them away without trying to conceal them. "You know my aunt," she began. "She was present, and she saw it, oh, with what eyes did she see it! Werther, last night I endured a sermon about my intercourse with you, and this morning, and I have had to hear you disparaged and degraded, and I could and might only half-defend you."

Every word she said went through my heart like a knife. She did not feel how compassionate it would have been to conceal all this from me, and now she went on to say what else would be gossiped, and what sorts of people would use it as a triumph.

How people would now gloat and rejoice over the punishment of my arrogance and my disdain of others, with which they have long been reproaching me. To hear all this from her, Wilhelm, in a tone of the warmest sympathy – I was annihilated, and I am still raging inside. I wish that someone would dare to throw it up to me, so that I could run my sword through his body; if I saw blood, I should feel relief. Oh, a hundred times I have seized a knife, to ease this burdened heart. It is said of a noble breed of horses that when they are fearfully heated and jaded, they instinctively bite open a vein, in order to help them get their breath. So I often feel, but I should like to open a vein that would procure me eternal freedom.

24th March

I have petitioned the court for my dismissal and hope to receive it, and you both will forgive me for not having first obtained your permission. Once and for all, I had to get away, and I know all the things you had in mind to say in order to induce me to remain, and so – feed this to my mother in a sweet syrup, for I cannot help myself, and she must put up with the fact that I cannot help her either. Of course it is bound to be painful to her. To see all at once the fine course halted, which her son had just begun as a road to Privy Councillor and Ambassador, and back to the stall with the little steed! Make of it what you will, and put together all the possible cases in which I could and should have remained; enough to say that I am going, and that you may know where I shall land, I'll tell you that Prince *** is here, who finds much pleasure in my company; hearing of my intentions, he has invited me to go with him to his estates, to spend the lovely springtime there. I have his promise that I am to be left to myself, and since we understand each other, up to a certain point, I'll take a chance and go with him.

19th April

For Your Information

Thanks, Wilhelm, for your two letters. I did not answer, because I let this sheet lie until my dismissal should have arrived from the court; I was afraid my mother might apply to the Minister and make my resolve more difficult. But now it is done, and my dismissal is here. I do not like to tell you how reluctantly it was given to me, and what the Minister writes to me: you would burst out into new lamentations. The Crown Prince sent me twenty-five ducats as a parting gift, with a note which moved me to tears; so I do not need to have my mother send me the money for which I lately asked.

5th May

Tomorrow I shall go from here, and since my birthplace lies only a few miles from the road, I will revisit that too, and will recall the days of old, so happily dreamt away. I will enter by the very gate through which my mother drove out with me, when she left the dear, familiar spot after the death of my father, to imprison me in her unbearable town. Adieu, Wilhelm, you shall have a report of my journey.

9th May

I completed the visit to my former home with all the veneration of a pilgrim, and some unexpected emotions came over me. By the great linden, which stands a mile from town on the road to S., I ordered a halt, got out and bade the postillion drive on, so as to taste on foot every recollection as something quite new, vivid and as my heart willed it. So there I stood under the linden which in former days of boyhood had been the goal and the limit of my strolls. How different! In those days I yearned in happy ignorance to get out into the unfamiliar world, where I hoped to find so much nourishment, so much enjoyment for my heart, wherewith to fill and to satisfy my aspiring, yearning bosom. Now I am returning from the wide world – O, my friend, with how many disappointed hopes, with how many ruined plans! I saw lying before me the mountains which had been so many thousands of times the object of my desires. For hours on end I could sit here, reaching over yonder with my longing, losing myself with all my soul in the woods and valleys which presented themselves to my eyes in such a pleasant vagueness, and then when I had to return at the appointed time, with what repugnance did I abandon that beloved spot! I approached the town, and all the old familiar summer houses were saluted, but the new ones were distasteful to me, as well as all the other alterations that had been made. I entered the gate, and at once and immediately I found myself again. I don't care to go into detail; charming as I found it, just so monotonous would it be in the recital. I had resolved to dwell on the marketplace, right next to our old house. As I walked along I observed that the school house, where an honest old woman had herded us together in childhood, was converted into a general shop. I recalled the uneasiness, the tears, the apathy, the heartfelt terror, which I had endured in that hole. There was not one step I took which was not noteworthy. A pilgrim in the Holy Land does not encounter as many stations of religious recollection, and his heart is scarcely as full of sacred emotion. One more item must serve for a thousand. I strolled down the stream as far as a certain farm; that had formerly been my course too, and the places where we boys would try to skip flat stones over the water the largest number of times. I recalled so vividly, when I stood still and looked after the flowing water, with what wonderful premonitions I used to follow its course, how thrilling I imagined the regions to be where it was bound, and how I had soon reached the limits of my imaginative power; and yet the water must go on, on and on, until I lost myself completely in the contemplation of an invisible distance. See, my good friend, just so confined and blissful were the glorious patriarchs! So childlike was their feeling, their poetry! When Ulysses speaks of the unmeasured sea and of the unending earth, that is so true, human, heartfelt, intimate and mysterious. What good does it do me that I can now parrot with every schoolboy the fact that it is round? Man needs but few clods of earth to base his happiness upon, less to cover his final rest.

Now I am here in the Prince's hunting lodge. It is quite easy to get along with this gentleman, for he is candid and simple. Strange people surround him whom I do not understand at all. They do not seem to be rascals, and yet they do not have the look of honest folk. Sometimes they seem honest to me, and yet I cannot trust them. Another thing that I regret is that he often speaks of things which he has only heard and read, always from the point of view which the other wanted to present to him.

Also, he prizes my intelligence and my talents more than he does this heart, which is after all my sole pride, which is the only source of everything I have, of all my force, all my bliss and all my misery. Oh, anyone can know what I know – only I possess my heart.

25th May

I had something in mind of which I was going to tell you nothing until it should be carried out; now that nothing is to come of it, it's perhaps just as well. I wanted to volunteer for war service; I have had that at heart for a long time. That was chiefly the reason why I followed the Prince here, he being a general in the service of ***. During a stroll I revealed my resolve to him; he advised me against it, and it would have had to be more a passion than a notion with me if I had not been willing to lend an ear to his reasoning.

11th June

Say what you will, I cannot stay here any longer. What am I to do here? Time hangs heavy. The Prince keeps me as well as one can, and yet I am not in my element. At bottom we have nothing in common. He is a man of sense, but of a very common sense; intercourse with him does not entertain me any more than the reading of a well-written book. I'll stay one week more, and then I shall resume my aimless roving. The best thing I have done here is to sketch. The Prince has a feeling for art, and would have a still stronger feeling if he were not hemmed in by his miserable scientism, and by the customary terminology. Sometimes I grit my teeth when guiding him through nature and art with warm imagination, and he suddenly blunders in with some stereotyped dictum and thinks he is doing just the right thing.

16th June

True, I am but a wanderer, a rover on earth! Are you more than that?

18th June

Where I am bound for? Let me tell you in confidence. For another fortnight I must stay here after all, and then I have persuaded myself that I wanted to visit the mines in ***; but actually there is nothing to that, and I only wish to get closer to Lotte, that is all. And I scoff at my own heart – and do its will.

29th July

No, it is all right! Everything is all right! I – her husband! O God who made me, if you had granted me that bliss, my whole life should be one continuous prayer. I offer no challenge, and forgive me these tears, forgive me my vain desires! She my wife! If I had clasped in my arms the dearest creature under the sun – a shiver goes through my whole body, Wilhelm, when Albert puts his arm around her slender waist.

And may I say this? Why not, Wilhelm? She would have been happier with me than with him! Oh, he is not the man to gratify all the desires of that heart. A certain lack of sensitivity, a lack – take it as you will; that his heart does not beat in sympathy at – oh! – at the passage in a loved book where our hearts, Lotte's and mine, came together; or in a hundred other cases, when it chances that we utter our feelings regarding an action or a third person. Dear Wilhelm! True, he loves her with all his heart, and what does such a love not deserve!

An unbearable person interrupted me. My tears are dried. I have lost the thread. Adieu.

4th August

I am not alone in this. All people are deceived in their hopes, duped in their expectations. I called on my good young woman under the linden. The oldest boy ran to meet me, and his cry of joy brought out his mother, who looked very depressed. Her first word was, "Good sir, alas, my Hans has died!" That was her youngest boy. I was silent. "And my husband," said she, "came back from Switzerland and brought nothing with him, and without the help of good people he would have had to beg his way out, for he had caught a fever on the way." I could say nothing to her, but gave something to the youngster; she begged me to accept some apples, which I did, and then left the place of sad recollection.

21st August

In the turn of a hand things change with me. Sometimes a joyous ray of life is about to dawn again, ah! – but only for a moment! When I lose myself like this in dreams, I cannot fight off the thought: what if Albert were to die? You would! Yes, she would – and then I run after that phantasm until it leads me to abysses from which I shrink back trembling.

If I go out of the gate along the road on which I drove for the first time to fetch Lotte for the dance, how very different that was! Everything, everything has gone by! No hint of that former world, not one pulse beat of the feeling I knew then. I feel as a spirit must, if it returned to the fire-gutted, ruined castle which as a thriving prince he had once built and furnished with all the attributes of splendour, and which at death he had hopefully bequeathed to his beloved son.

3rd September

Sometimes I do not understand how any other *can* love her, is permitted to love her, since I love her so exclusively, so deeply, so fully, and neither know nor have anything but her!

4th September

Yes, it is so. As nature inclines towards the autumn, so it is becoming autumn in me and about me. My leaves are turning yellow, and the leaves of the neighbouring trees have already fallen. Did I not write you once about a peasant lad, just after I came here? Now I have enquired about him in Wahlheim; they said he had been harshly dismissed, and nobody claimed to know anything more about him. Yesterday I met him by chance on my way to another village; I spoke to him, and he told me his story, which touched me doubly and trebly, as you will readily understand when I retail it to you. Yet why all this, and why don't I keep to myself what frightens and wounds me? Why do I sadden you too? Why do I keep giving you opportunities to pity me and to scold me? So be it, that too may be a part of my fate!

With a quiet melancholy, in which I seemed to detect some timidity, the young man answered my first questions, but very soon more candidly, as if all at once he knew himself and me again, he confessed his failings, bewailed his unhappiness. Could I, my friend, refer every one of his words to your judgement! He admitted, indeed he recounted with a kind of enjoyment and the happiness of remembrance, that his passion for his mistress had increased in him day by day, so that at last he did not know what he was doing, nor, as he expressed it, where to turn. He had been unable to eat or drink or sleep, and had felt choked; he had done what he should not and had forgotten what he was ordered to do, and it had been as if he were pursued by an evil spirit; until one day, when he knew she was in an upstairs room, he had followed her, or rather had been drawn after her. As she had lent no ear to his pleading, he had tried to take possession of her by force; he did not know what had come over him, and he called God to witness that his intentions towards her had always been honourable, and that he had desired nothing more earnestly than that she would marry him, that she might spend her life with him. When he had spoken thus for a while, he began to hesitate, like a man who has something more to say and does not dare to utter it; at last he also admitted to me, shyly, all the little liberties she had allowed him, and how close she had let him come to her. He broke off two or three times, repeating the most animated protestations that he was not saying this to blacken her, as he put it, that he loved and valued her as before, that such words had never crossed his lips, and that he was only saying this to me in order to convince me that he was not a wholly perverted and unreasonable person – and here, my friend, I strike up my old song again, the one I shall sing eternally: if I could only place this man before you as he stood before me, as he still stands before me! If I could tell you everything properly, so that you should feel how I sympathize with his fate, and must do so! But enough: since you also know my fate, and me as well, then you know only too well what draws me to all those who are unhappy, and especially to this unhappy one.

Now that I read this page over, I see that I have forgotten to tell the end of the story, which however is easy to imagine. She resisted him; her brother came up, who had long hated him and had long wanted him out of the house, because he feared that a new marriage would make his sister withdraw from his children the inheritance which right now raises his hopes, since she is childless. The brother had kicked him out of the house at once and made such a fuss over the affair that the woman, even if she had wished, could not have taken him back. Now, he said, she had hired another servant, and on his account too, it was said, she had fallen out with her brother, and it was positively asserted that she was going to marry him, but he was firmly resolved not to see that happen.

What I am telling you is not exaggerated, not sentimentalized, and indeed I may well say that I have told it feebly, feebly, while I have coarsened it by reporting it with our conventional moral words.

So then, this love, this loyalty, this passion, is no poetic invention. It is alive, and in its complete genuineness it exists amid that class of people whom we call uncultured, whom we call crude. We refined ones – refined until there is nothing left! Read this story with reverence, I beg you. I am quiet today as I write this down; you see by my handwriting that I am not smearing and splashing as usual. Read, my dear fellow, and think as you do so that it is also the story of your friend. Yes, so it was with me, so it will be with me, and I am not half as good, not half as resolute as that poor, unhappy fellow, with whom I am almost afraid to compare myself.

5th September

She had written a note to her husband, whom business affairs had kept for some time in the country. It began, "Dearest and best, come as soon as you can. I shall be overjoyed to see you back." A friend who came in brought word that certain circumstances would keep him from returning so soon. The

little note was not sent and got into my hands that evening.
I read it and smiled: she asked me why. "What a divine
gift is the imagination," I cried, "for a moment I was able
to conceive that this was written to me." She dropped the
subject, seeming displeased, and I said no more.

6th September

It was hard for me to resolve to put away the plain blue dress
coat in which I had my first dance with Lotte, but it finally
became too shabby. But I also had a new one made that was
just like its predecessor, with collar and lapels, and with it
again a yellow waistcoat and trousers.

Yet the effect is not precisely the same. I don't know – I
believe that in time I shall get to like this one better.

12th September

She was out of town for some days, having gone to fetch
Albert. Today I entered her room, she came towards me, and
I kissed her hand, overjoyed.

A canary left the mirror and flew to her shoulder. "A new
friend," she said, enticing it to perch on her hand, "it was
bought for my little ones. It is just too sweet! Look at it! If
I give it bread, it flutters its wings and pecks so daintily. It
kisses me too, look!"

As she held out her mouth to the little creature, it pressed
into the sweet lips as charmingly as if it could have felt the
bliss it was enjoying.

"It shall kiss you too," she said, handing the bird to me.
The tiny beak made its way from her lips to mine, and the
pecking contact was like a breath, a faint suggestion of a
lovely pleasure.

"Its kiss," I said, "is not quite without greed: it seeks
nourishment and returns unsatisfied after an empty caress."

"It will also eat out of my mouth," she said. She fed it some crumbs with her lips, whose smiles expressed the joys of an innocently shared love.

I turned my face away. She should not do it! Should not goad my imagination with these pictures of heavenly innocence and blissfulness, not awaken my heart out of the slumber into which it is rocked at times by the indifference of life! And why not? She has such confidence in me! She knows how much I love her!

15th September

It is infuriating, Wilhelm, that there are human beings without feeling or appreciation for the few things on earth that still have some value. You know the walnut trees under which I sat with Lotte at the house of the honest pastor of St ***, those magnificent trees which, God knows, filled my soul with the greatest joy! How familiar they made the parsonage, how cool! And how splendid the branches were! And recollection extending back to the honest pastor couple that planted them so many years ago. The schoolmaster often told us one of their names, which he had heard from his grandfather – and he is said to have been such a good man, and his memory was always sacred to me under those trees. I tell you, the schoolmaster had tears in his eyes as we spoke yesterday of their having been cut down – cut down! I could go mad, I could murder the cur that struck the first blow. I, who could grieve myself to death if such a pair of trees stood in my yard and one of them died of old age, I have to see this done. My dear fellow, there is one compensation all the same! What a thing is human feeling! The whole village is murmuring, and I hope the pastor's wife will be made to feel, by a lack of butter and eggs and of other marks of confidence, the wound she has dealt her village. For it is she, the wife of the new pastor (our old one has died too), a lean, sickly creature, who has every reason to take no interest in the world, for no one takes an interest in her. A silly fool she is, who makes pretensions to being learned, who meddles with the problem of which books of the Bible are genuine, works a great deal at the new-fashioned

moral and critical re-evaluation of Christian ethics, and shrugs
her shoulders at Lavater's enthusiasms, and whose health is
thoroughly broken down, for which reason she has no joy on
God's earth. Nor would it have been possible for any other
creature to cut down my walnut trees. See, I can't get over it! Just
imagine, the falling leaves make her yard disorderly and dank,
the trees rob her of daylight and when the nuts are ripe the boys
throw stones at them: that gets on her nerves, that disturbs her
deep meditations when she is weighing Kennicott, Semler and
Michaelis* one against the other. When I saw that the people
in the village, especially the old ones, were so discontented,
I said, "Why did you permit it?" They said, "If the mayor is
willing, here in the country, what can be done?" But one thing
was rightly done. The mayor and the pastor, who was hoping
to get some advantage from the silly notions of his wife – which
don't make his soup any more savoury – thought they would
divide the profit, but the treasury got wind of it and said, "Hand
it over!" For it still had old claims to that part of the parsonage
where the trees stood, and it sold them to the highest bidder.
They are down! Oh, if I were the prince! I would see to it that
the pastor's wife, the mayor and the treasury – prince! Well, if
I were the prince, what would I care about the trees in my land?

10th October

If I merely see her black eyes, I feel better at once! Look, and
what vexes me is that Albert does not seem to be as happy
as he – hoped – as I – think I should be – if – I am not fond
of writing dashes, but in this case I have no other way of
expressing myself – and I think it is plain enough.

12th October

Ossian has displaced Homer in my heart. What a world it is
into which the glorious one leads me! To stroll across the heath,
with the gale roaring around me, which leads in steaming mists

the spirits of our fathers through the vague light of the moon. To hear from yonder mountains, amid the roar of the forest stream, the half-obliterated groaning of the spirits from the caves, and the lamentations of the girl who is grieving herself to death, hovering about the four moss-covered, grass-grown gravestones of her beloved, fallen noble. Then when I find him, the grey-haired, roving bard, who seeks on the spacious heath the footprints of his forebears, and – ah! – finds their gravestones, and then looks wailing towards the good evening star which conceals itself in the rolling waves of the ocean, and the past ages come to life in the soul of the hero, days when a friendly ray illumined the perils of the brave, and the moon shone upon their beribboned ship on its victorious return. When I read on his brow his deep distress, see this last forsaken hero totter in complete exhaustion towards the grave, noting how he keeps drinking in ever new, painfully glowing joys in the enfeebled presence of the shades of his departed ones, and how he looks towards the cold earth, the tall, waving grass, and exclaims, "The wanderer will come, who knew me in my beauty, and will ask, 'Where is the singer, Fingal's excellent son? His footstep goes over my grave, and he asks in vain after me on the earth.'" – O my friend! I would like to draw my sword like an ancient man-at-arms, free my prince at one stroke from the quivering torment of a life of slow death, and send my own soul after the liberated demigod.

19th October

Oh, this void! This fearful void which I feel here in my breast! I often think to myself: if you could press her just once to this heart, just once, then this entire void would be filled.

26th October

Yes, it is becoming certain to me, friend, certain and ever more certain, that little importance is attached to the existence of any being, very little. A woman friend came to see Lotte, and I went into the adjoining room to get a book, but could not read, and then I took a pen to do some writing. I heard them speaking quietly; they were telling each other unimportant matters, town gossip: this girl is getting married, that one is sick, very sick. "She has a hacking cough, her face is only skin and bones, and she has fainting spells; I wouldn't give a penny for her life," said the one. "And Mr N.N. is in a bad way too," said Lotte. "He is already bloated," said the other. And my vivid imagination took me to the bedside of these poor people; I saw with what reluctance they were turning their backs upon life, how they – Wilhelm! And my little ladies were talking about it as people do talk about the fact that a stranger is dying. And when I look about me and survey the room, and around me are Lotte's dresses and Albert's writings and these furnishings, with which I am on such friendly terms, including this inkwell, and I think, "See what you mean to this household! All in all. Your friends honour you! You are often a joy to them, and to your heart it seems as if that joy were indispensable, and yet – if you were to go, if you parted from their circle? Would they, and how long would they feel the void that the loss of you would inflict upon their destiny? How long?" – oh, man is so transitory that even where he finds the only evidence for his existence, even where his presence makes its only true impression, namely, in the memory, in the souls of his loved ones, even there he must be extinguished and disappear, and how quickly!

27th October

Often I would like to rend my breast and knock in my brain, seeing that people can be so little to each other. Ah, the love, joy, warmth and rapture which I cannot bestow will not be given to me by the other, and even with a whole heart full of bliss I shall not delight one who stands before me cold and sapless.

Evening

I have so much, and my feeling for her engulfs it all; I have so much, and without her I find everything turned into nothing.

30th October

If I have not been a hundred times on the point of flinging my arms about her! The great God knows how it feels to see so much loveliness go criss-cross before me and be forbidden to reach for it, and yet reaching for things is the most natural impulse in man. Don't children reach for everything they see? And I?

3rd November

God knows, I often get into bed with the desire, indeed at times with the hope, of not awaking again, and in the morning I open my eyes, see the sun again and am wretched. Oh that I could be capricious, could put the blame on the weather, on a third party, on a frustrated undertaking, then I would only have to bear half the unbearable burden of ill humour. But woe is me! I feel too plainly that all the guilt is mine alone – no, not guilt! Bad enough that in me the source of all my misery lies concealed, as formerly the source of all my joys. Am I not still the very one who formerly revelled in all the fullness of his feeling, whose every step was followed by paradise, who had a heart that could lovingly embrace an entire world? And that heart is dead now, no raptures issue from it any more, my eyes are dried up, and my thoughts, no longer regaled with refreshing tears, draw my brow into anxious folds. I suffer much, for I have lost what was the sole rapture of my life, that holy, animating force with which I created worlds all about me – it is gone! When I gaze out of my window towards the distant height, seeing how the morning sun breaks through the mist above it and lights up the quiet valley meadow, and the gentle stream meanders towards me between its leafless willows – oh, when that glorious natural scene stands before me as lifeless as a chromo, and all this rapture cannot pump one drop of bliss from my heart up into my brain, and this whole fellow stands before the countenance of God like a dried-up well or a leaky bucket. I have often flung myself on the ground and begged God for tears, as a ploughman prays for rain when the sky is brazen above him and around him the earth is parching.

But alas, I feel that God does not give rain and sunshine in response to our impetuous requests, and those former days whose memory torments me, why were they so blissful? Why else than because I awaited his spirit with patience, and welcomed the rapture which he poured over me with undivided, deeply grateful heart!

8th November

She has rebuked my excesses! Ah, but so lovably! My excesses, whereby I sometimes let myself be seduced by a glass of wine into drinking a bottle. "Don't do it!" she said. "Think of Lotte!"

"Think!" said I. "Do you need to bid me do that? I think – I don't think! You are always present to my soul. Today I was sitting at the spot where you lately dismounted from the carriage—" She spoke of something else, so as not to let me enlarge upon the subject. Best of friends, I am done for! She can do with me whatever she will.

15th November

I thank you, Wilhelm, for your heartfelt sympathy, for your well-meant advice, and beg you to be calm. Let me endure to the end: for all my wearisomeness I still have force enough to hold out. I honour religion, as you know, and I realize that it is a staff to many a weary wanderer, refreshment to the languishing. Only – can it, must it be so to everyone? If you behold the great world, you will see thousands who did not find it so, thousands who will never find it so, whether preached to them or not – and must it be so to me? Does not even the Son of God say that those would be around him whom the Father has given to him? What if I am not given to him? What if the Father wants to keep me for Himself, as my heart tells me? I beg you not to misinterpret this; do not see a mockery in these innocent words: it is my whole soul that I am laying before you – else I should wish I had held my peace, just as I am reluctant to say anything about all those matters of which everyone knows as little as I do. What is human destiny other than to endure your measure of suffering, drink your cup to the dregs? And if the God from heaven found the cup too bitter for his human lips, why should I exalt myself and act as if it tasted sweet to me? And why should I be ashamed, in the terrible moment when my whole existence is trembling between being and not-being, when the past shines like a flash of lightning over the dark abyss of the future, and everything about me is sinking, and the world going to destruction with me – isn't it then the voice of the creature which is being driven back into itself, fails to find a self and irresistibly tumbles to its fall, that groans from the inner depths of its vainly aspiring powers, "My God! My God! Why hast thou forsaken me?" And should I be ashamed of that saying, should I be afraid of that moment, seeing that he who rolls up the heavens like a robe did not escape it?

21st November

She does not see, she does not feel, that she is preparing a poison which will destroy me and herself, and I sip to the bottom, with fullest enjoyment, the cup she hands me for my ruin. Of what avail is the kind gaze with which she often – often? – no, not often, but sometimes looks at me, the complaisance with which she receives an involuntary expression of my emotion, the sympathy with my suffering that is delineated on her brow?

Yesterday, as I was departing, she held out her hand and said, "Adieu, dear Werther!" Dear Werther! It was the first time that she had called me "dear", and it sent a shiver all through me. I have repeated it to myself a hundred times, and last evening, as I was about to go to bed and was chatting about all sorts of things with myself, I said all at once, "Good night, dear Werther!" and afterwards I had to laugh at myself.

22nd November

I cannot pray, "Let me have her!" and yet she often seems to me to be mine. I cannot pray, "Give her to me!" for she belongs to another. I indulge in all sorts of quibbles about my griefs; if I let myself go, the result would be a whole litany of contradictions.

24th November

She feels what I am suffering. Today her gaze penetrated deeply into my soul. I found her alone; I said nothing, and she looked at me. And I no longer saw in her the charming beauty, no longer the shining of her excellent mind; all that had vanished before my eyes. A much more glorious gaze stirred me, full of the expression of the deepest sympathy, of the sweetest compassion. Why could I not fling myself at her feet? Why could I not weep my answer on her neck with a thousand kisses? She took refuge in her piano, and with sweet and low voice she breathed out tones in harmony with her playing. Never have I seen her lips so charming: it was as if they opened in a famishing desire to sip in those sweet sounds that welled forth from the piano, and as if only the mysterious echo responded from that pure mouth – oh, if I could only tell you how it was! I resisted no longer, bowed my head and vowed: "Never will I dare, you lips, to press a kiss upon you, on which the spirits of heaven hover – and yet – I want – ha! Do you see, that stands before my soul like a barrier – this bliss – and then, lost for ever to expiate that sin – sin?

26th November

Sometimes I tell myself: your fate is unique; consider all others fortunate – no other has ever been so tormented. Then I read a poet of past times, and it is as if I were looking into my own heart. I have so much to endure! Ah, have people before me ever been as wretched as I?

30th November

It is, it *is* my fate not to come to my senses! Wherever I go, I encounter some apparition which robs me of all composure. Today! O fate! O humanity!

I was strolling along the stream in the noon hour, having no desire to eat. All was desolate, a moist, chill west wind blew down from the mountain, and the grey rain clouds were drifting into the valley. From afar I saw a man in a worn green coat, who was crawling about among the rocks and seemed to be seeking herbs. When I came closer, and he turned around at the noise I made, I saw a most interesting face, in which a quiet sorrow was the main feature, but which otherwise expressed nothing but a good, straightforward mind; his black locks were put up in two rolls with hairpins, the rest being braided into a heavy plait that hung down his back. As his clothing seemed to me to indicate a man of lowly station, I thought he would not take it amiss if I paid attention to his occupation, and so I asked him what he was seeking. "I am seeking flowers," he answered with a deep sigh, "and I find none."

"Nor is this the season," I said with a smile.

"There are so many flowers," he said, coming down to me. "In my garden there are roses and two kinds of honeysuckle, one of which my father gave me, and they grow like weeds; I have been looking for them for two days, and I can't find them. Out yonder, too, there are always flowers, yellow and blue and red ones, and the centaury has a pretty little flower. I can't find any of them."

I saw that something was wrong, and so I asked a roundabout question: "What do you want to do with the flowers?" A strange, twitching smile puckered his face. "If you will not give me away," he said, putting a finger on his lips, "I have promised my sweetheart a bouquet."

"That is nice," I said.

"Oh," said he, "she has lots of other things, she is rich."

"And yet she loves your bouquet," I responded.

"Oh!" he continued. "She has jewels and a crown."

"Why, what is her name?"

"If the States-General would pay me," he replied, "I'd be a different person! Yes, there once was a time when I was so happy! Now it's all over with me. I am now..." A moist glance towards the sky expressed everything.

"So you were happy?" I asked.

"Oh, I wish I were again like that!" said he. "At that time I was as happy, as merry, as unburdened as a fish in water!"

"Heinrich!" called an old woman who came along the path. "Heinrich, where are you hiding? We have been looking for you everywhere, come to lunch!"

"Is that your son?" I asked, approaching her.

"Indeed, my poor son," she replied. "God has given me a heavy cross to bear."

"How long has he been so?" I asked. "In this calm state," she said, "he has been for half a year now. Thank God that it is no worse than this; before that he was raving for a whole year and lay chained up in the madhouse. Now he harms nobody, only he is always having to do with kings and emperors. He was such a good, quiet person, wrote a fine hand and helped to support me; all at once he grew melancholy, fell into a high fever, which turned into madness, and now he is as you see him. If I were to tell you, sir—"

I broke in upon the stream of her words by asking, "What kind of a time was it that he praises so, saying that he was so happy then, so well off?"

"The foolish fellow!" she cried with a compassionate smile. "He means the time when he was out of his mind, he is always praising that; that is the time when he was in the madhouse, when he knew nothing about himself..." This struck me like a thunderclap, and I put a coin in her hand and left her in haste.

"When you were happy!" I exclaimed, walking rapidly towards the town. "When you felt as cheerful as a fish in water!" God in heaven! Have you made that to be the fate of men, that they are not happy until they have acquired some sense and then lose it again? Poor wretch! And yet how I envy your clouded mind, the confusion of thought in which you are languishing! You go out in the hope of picking flowers for your queen – in the winter – and mourn because you find none, and fail to understand why you can find none. And I – and I go out without hope, without purpose, and return home the same as when I went. You dream of what a man you would be if the States-General paid you. Happy creature! Able as you are to ascribe your lack of happiness to an earthly obstacle. You do not feel! You do not feel that in your ravaged heart, in your deranged brain, your misery lies, from which you cannot be freed by all the kings of the earth.

"That man should die disconsolate who scoffs at a sufferer journeying towards the remotest wellspring, which will augment his illness, make his death more painful! Or who looks down upon the hard-pressed heart which, in order to rid itself of pangs of conscience, and to lay aside the sufferings of his soul, makes a pilgrimage to the Holy Sepulchre. Every step which cuts through his shoes on his pathless way is a drop of balm for the terrified soul, and with every completed day's journey his heart is relieved of many distresses as it lays itself down. Have you a right to call that a delusion, you phrasemongers on your beds of ease? Delusion! O God, you see my tears! Having created man with poverty enough, must you also endow him with brothers who would rob him of even the little he had, of his bit of trust in you, in you, you all-loving one? For man's trust in a healing root, in the tears of the grapevine, what is that but trust in you, trust that you have put into all that surrounds us the curative and alleviating force of which we have an hourly need? Father whom I do not know! Father who once filled my whole soul, and who has now turned his countenance away from me! Call me to you! Keep silence no longer! Your silence will not sustain this thirsting soul – and would a man, a father, be able to show anger, if his unexpectedly returning son should fall upon his neck and cry, "I am here again, my father! Be not angry that I am cutting short the journey which it was your will that I should endure still longer. The world is everywhere the same, reward and joy following upon effort and toil, but what does that mean to me? I only feel content where you are, and in your presence I wish to suffer and to enjoy." And you, dear heavenly Father, should you thrust him from you?

1st December

Wilhelm! The man about whom I wrote to you, that happily unhappy man, was a clerk employed by Lotte's father, and a passion for her which he cherished, concealed and revealed, and which caused his dismissal from the steward's service, made him demented. Feel as you see these prosy words with what a turmoil this story gripped me, when Albert told it to me just as calmly as you will perhaps read it.

4th December

I beg of you – you see, it is all up with me, I can bear it no longer! Today I was sitting with her – sitting, and she was playing on her piano, various melodies, and all that expression! All! All! What would you? Her little sister was on my knee dressing her doll. Tears came into my eyes. I bent down, and her wedding ring struck my gaze – my tears flowed – and all at once she dropped into that old, divinely sweet melody, all of a sudden, and through my soul passed a feeling of consolation, and a recollection of things past, of the times when I had heard that song, of the gloomy intervals of vexation, of frustrated hopes, and then – I walked up and down the room, my heart suffocating under all that flooded into it. "For God's sake," I said, going up to her in an impetuous outburst, "for God's sake, stop!" She stopped and stared at me. "Werther," she said with a smile that pierced my soul, "Werther, you are very sick, even your favourite dishes disagree with you. Go now! I beg you, calm yourself." I tore myself away from her, and – God! – you see my misery, and you will end it.

6th December

How that figure pursues me! Waking and dreaming it fills my whole soul! Here, when I close my eyes, here in my brow, where the power of inner vision unites, are her black eyes. Here! I cannot put it into words for you. If I close my eyes, there they are; like an ocean, like an abyss they lie still before me, in me, filling all the thoughts within my brow.

What is man, the eulogized demigod? Does he not lack force at the very point where he needs it most? And when he soars upwards in joy, or sinks down in suffering, is he not checked in both, is he not returned again to the dull, cold sphere of awareness, just when he was longing to lose himself in the fullness of the infinite?

The Editor to the Reader

HOW DEEPLY I SHOULD WISH that of the last remarkable days of our friend so many personal testimonials had remained to us that I should not need to interrupt the sequence of his posthumous letters with my own narrative.

I have been at pains to collect precise information from the lips of those who could be well apprized of his story; it is simple, and all the accounts of it, apart from a few details, agree with each other; only with regard to the states of mind of the actors do opinions differ, and judgements are divided.

What is left for us save to narrate conscientiously what we have been able to learn by dint of repeated, diligent inquiry, to insert the letters left behind by the departing one, and not to disregard even the tiniest scrap of paper; especially since it is so difficult to discover the true and peculiar motives of even a single action, if it takes place among persons not of the common stamp.

Discontent and moroseness had taken deeper and deeper root in Werther's soul, becoming more firmly intertwined, and had gradually filled his entire being. The harmony of his mind was wholly destroyed, and an inner fever and fury, which threw all the forces of his nature into confusion, produced the most contradictory effects and finally left him with nothing but exhaustion, from which he strove to free himself even more anxiously than he had previously struggled with all his other trials. The intimidation of his heart consumed all other forces of his mind, his vivacity and his perceptiveness; he became a sad figure in society, steadily more unhappy, and his injustice to others grew with his unhappiness. At least this is said by Albert's friends; they maintain that Werther was not able to judge the conduct of a quiet man who had finally become possessed of a long-desired happiness, and who sought to preserve this happiness for the future, Werther being a man who consumed his entire fortune, as it were, each day, whereupon each evening saw him suffer pain and want. Albert, they say, had not altered in that short time, he continued to be the same person that Werther had known from the outset, and that he had so greatly esteemed and honoured. Albert loved Lotte more than anything else, he was proud of her, and he likewise wished to see her recognized by everyone as the most glorious of creatures. Was he then to be blamed if he desired to avert even the least shadow of a suspicion, if at that stage he had no wish to share this precious possession with anyone, even in the most innocent fashion? They admit that Albert often left his wife's room when Werther was with her, but not out of hatred or aversion towards his friend, only because he felt that the latter was oppressed by his presence.

Lotte's father had been seized by an ailment which kept him indoors; he sent her his carriage, and she drove out to see him. It was a fine winter day; the first snow had fallen heavily, covering the whole landscape.

Werther followed after her on the next day, in order to escort her back, in case Albert did not come to fetch her.

The bright weather was unable to have much influence on his melancholy mood: a dull weight burdened his soul, the pictures of sadness had established themselves firmly within him, and his spirit knew no activity save to shift from one painful thought to another.

As he lived in eternal conflict with himself, so the state of others seemed to him all the more dubious and confused; he believed that he had disturbed the fine relationship between Albert and his wife, and he reproached himself for this, feeling at the same time a secret anger against her husband.

His thoughts touched again upon this subject as he walked along. "Yes, yes," he said to himself, secretly gritting his teeth, "that is the familiar, amiable, tender association, sharing in all things, the calm, lasting loyalty! Satiety and indifference, that is what it is! Does not any miserable business matter attract him more than his precious, delicious wife? Does he know how to appreciate his good fortune? Does he know how to esteem her as she deserves? He has her; all right, he has her – I know that, as I also know something else, and I believe myself accustomed to the idea, but it will yet make me mad, it will yet deprive me of my life – and has his friendship with me held water? Does he not already see in my attachment to Lotte an invasion of his rights, in my attentiveness to her a silent reproach? I know very well, I feel, that he does not like to see me, that he wishes my removal, that my presence is burdensome to him."

Repeatedly he checked his rapid pace, often he stood still, seeming to be about to turn back, but again and again he redirected his course forward, and in the midst of these thoughts and soliloquies he at last reached the hunting lodge, against his will as it were.

He entered the door and asked about Lotte and her father, finding the house in some commotion. The oldest boy told him that an accident had taken place over in Wahlheim, that a farmer had been slain. This made no impression upon him. He entered the living room and found Lotte trying to dissuade her father, who despite his illness wanted to go over and investigate the affair on the spot. The slayer was as yet unknown, but the victim had been found in the morning before the door of the house, and there were suspicions: the victim was the servant of a widow who had previously had another man in her service, whom discord had driven from her house.

When Werther heard this, he started up vehemently. "Is it possible!" he exclaimed. "I must go over there, I can't wait one minute." He hurried towards Wahlheim, every recollection came to life in him, and he did not doubt for a moment that the crime had been committed by that man with whom he had had a number of talks, and whom he had come to like so much.

As he had to go through the lindens to get to the tavern where they had deposited the body, he was horrified at the sight of the spot he had loved so much. The threshold on which the neighbour's children had so often played was sullied with blood. Love and loyalty, the fairest human feelings, had turned into violence and murder. The stately trees stood bare and covered with frost, the fine hedges which arched over the low wall of the churchyard were denuded, and the gravestones, covered with snow, were visible through the gaps.

As he approached the tavern, before which the whole village was assembled, suddenly a clamour arose. From afar a troop of armed men was seen, and everyone cried that they were bringing the slayer. Werther looked in that direction and was not long in doubt. Yes! It was the servant who had loved the widow so much, and whom Werther had encountered some time before, going about in his silent wrath, in his hidden despair.

"What have you done, unhappy man!" exclaimed Werther, as he went towards the prisoner. The latter looked at him quietly, and in silence, and finally replied quite calmly, "No one shall have her, and she will have no one." They led the captive into the tavern, and Werther hurried away.

As a result of this frightful, violent contact, everything in his nature had been thrown into turmoil. For a moment he was suddenly torn out of his sadness, his discontent, his apathetic resignation; sympathy took hold of him invincibly, and an unspeakable desire came over him to save that man. He felt him to be so unhappy, he found him so guiltless even as a criminal, he put himself so profoundly in his situation, that he was confident he could persuade others as well. Already he felt a desire to be able to speak for the man, already the most animated plea was on his lips, he hurried towards the hunting lodge, and on the way he could not refrain from uttering under his breath all the arguments he was going to present to the steward.

When he entered the room, he found Albert there, and this vexed him for a moment, but he soon composed himself again and recited his ideas to the steward with ardour. The latter shook his head a couple of times, and although Werther brought forward with the greatest vivacity, passion and truth all that a man could say in exculpation of another, yet the steward, as can easily be imagined, was not moved by it. On the contrary, he did not let our friend finish, opposed him strongly and rebuked him for taking the side of an assassin! He showed him that in this fashion all law would be annulled, all the security of the state destroyed, and he also added that in such an affair he could do nothing without taking upon himself the greatest responsibility: everything, he said, must be done in order and follow the prescribed course.

Werther did not yet admit defeat, but he merely requested the steward to look the other way if the man should be helped to escape. This too the steward rejected. Albert, who finally entered into the conversation, likewise sided with the older man. Werther was outvoted, and in fearful suffering he set out again, after the steward had said to him repeatedly, "No, he cannot be saved!"

How sharply these words must have struck him we see from a little note which was found among his papers, and which was undoubtedly written on that same day.

You cannot be saved, unhappy man! I see clearly that we cannot be saved.

What Albert had at last said about the case of the prisoner in the presence of the steward had been most repugnant to Werther: he thought he had observed in it some resentment against himself, and although upon repeated reflection it did not escape his keen mind that both men might be in the right, yet it was as if he must renounce his own inmost existence in order to confess it, in order to admit it.

We find among his papers a page which refers to this, and which perhaps expresses his entire relation to Albert:

Of what avail that I say to myself, over and over, that he is good and honest: it tears my entrails apart, I cannot be just.

Since it was a mild evening, and the weather was beginning to encourage a thaw, Lotte walked back on foot with Albert. On the way they looked about them now and then, just as if they missed Werther's escort. Albert began to speak of him, censuring him while at the same time doing him justice. He touched upon his unhappy passion, wishing that it might be possible to get him away from there. "I wish that for our sakes too," he said, "and I beg you," he went on, "take measures to give his behaviour towards you a different direction and to reduce the frequency of his visits. People are beginning to notice, and I know that in some places it has been discussed." Lotte was silent, and Albert seemed to have felt her silence; at least from that time on he did not speak of Werther to her again, and if she mentioned him, he would drop the conversation or turn it in some other direction.

The vain attempt which Werther had made to rescue the unfortunate man was the last flare of the flame of a failing candle; he sank all the deeper into pain and inactivity; especially, he grew almost beside himself when he heard that he would perhaps even be summoned to testify against the man, who had now had recourse to denial.

All the disagreeable things that had ever come his way in his active life, his vexation while with the embassy, all else in which he had failed, all that had ever wounded him, kept going back and forth within his soul. He seemed to himself justified in his inactivity by all this, he seemed cut off from all future prospects, incapable of getting anywhere a handhold such as one uses on the affairs of common life, and so in the end, wholly surrendered to his strange feeling, his mode of thinking and an endless passion, in the eternal monotony of an unhappy association with the lovable and loved creature whose calm he was disturbing, tearing at his own powers, which he wore down without purpose or prospect, he moved ever closer to a melancholy end.

The strongest evidence of his bewilderment and passion, his unquiet striving and driving, his weariness of life, is some letters left by him, which we will insert here.

12th December

Dear Wilhelm, I am in such a state as those unfortunates must have been, of whom it was believed that they were driven about by an evil spirit. Sometimes I feel a seizure: it is not fear, not desire – it is an inner and unknown storm which threatens to rend my breast, which squeezes my throat shut! Woe, woe! And then I rove about in the fearful nocturnal scenes of this hostile winter season.

Yesterday evening I felt I must go out. A sudden thaw had set in, and I had heard that the river had overflowed, that all the brooks were swollen, and that from Wahlheim down, my beloved valley was flooded! I ran out after eleven at night. A terrible spectacle, to see the raging floods, descending from the rocks, swirling in the moonlight, cover fields and meadows and hedges and all, and the broad valley in both directions turned into a surging lake in the roar of the wind! And then when the moon came out again and rested above the dark cloud, and out in front of me the waters rolled and rang in the fearfully magnificent reflection: then a shiver came over me, and once more a longing! Ah, with open arms I stood facing an abyss, and murmured, "Down! Down!" and was lost in the rapture of having my torments, my suffering go sweeping down there! surging along with the waves! Oh! And you were unable to lift your feet from the ground and put an end to all torments! My clock has not yet run down, I feel that! O Wilhelm, how gladly I would have given all my human existence in order to rend the clouds with that gale, or to take hold of the flood waters! Ha! And will the imprisoned one not enjoy that rapture, some time?

And as I looked mournfully down at a spot where I had rested under a willow with Lotte, during a walk on a hot day – that too was flooded, and I could barely recognize the willow! Wilhelm! "And her meadows," I thought, "the lands around the hunting lodge! How ruined now is our summer arbour by the rushing river," I thought. And the sunshine of the past looked in at me, as a prisoner dreams a dream of flocks, meadows and dignities! I stood still! I do not rebuke myself, for I have courage to die. I might have – now I am sitting here like an old crone who gleans firewood from fence posts and begs her bread, in order for one moment to lengthen and to lighten her fading, joyless existence.

14th December

What is this, my friend? I shrink from myself! Is not my love for her the holiest, purest, most brotherly love? Have I ever felt a culpable desire in my soul? I will make no protestations – and now, dreams! Oh how true was the feeling of men who ascribed such contrary effects to alien powers! Last night! I tremble to say it, but I held her in my arms, firmly pressed to my breast, and covered her mouth, which murmured love, with unending kisses; my eyes were afloat in the intoxication of hers! God! Am I culpable, that even now I feel a bliss in recalling those ardent joys in all their intensity? Lotte! Lotte! And it is all over with me! My thoughts blur, for a week now I have had no more self-control, my eyes are full of tears. I am nowhere content, and everywhere content, I wish nothing, demand nothing. It would be better for me if I went away.

The resolve to quit the world had, at this time and under such circumstances, gained more and more power over Werther's soul. Since his return to Lotte, this had always been his final prospect and hope, but he had told himself that it should not be an overhasty or precipitate deed: he would take this step with the soundest conviction, with a resoluteness of the greatest possible quietude.

His doubts, his struggle with himself, are evident from a note which is probably the beginning of a letter to Wilhelm, and which was found undated among his papers.

Her presence, her fate, her sympathy with my fate, is squeezing the last remaining tears out of my desiccated brain.

To lift the curtain and step behind it! That is all! And why this delay and lagging? Because we don't know how things look over yonder? And we don't return? And because that is a trait of our mind, to surmise confusion and darkness in that about which we know nothing definite.

At last he became more and more akin to and befriended with this sad idea, and his resolve grew firm and irrevocable, of which evidence is given by the following ambiguous letter which he wrote to his friend.

20th December

I owe thanks to your love, Wilhelm, for taking my words as you did. Yes, you are right: it would be better for me if I went away. Your proposal that I rejoin you does not entirely suit me; at least I should like to make a detour, especially since we hope to have lasting frost and good roads. And I like it very much that you want to come to fetch me; just wait another fortnight, and look for one more letter from me with further information. It is needful that nothing should be picked before it is ripe. And a fortnight more or less can do much. Tell my mother this: that she should pray for her son, and that I beg her forgiveness for all the distress I have caused her. That had to be my fate, to sadden those to whom I owed it to bring happiness. Farewell, my dearest friend! All the blessings of heaven upon you! Farewell!

What went on in Lotte's soul during this time, how she felt towards her husband, towards her unhappy friend, we scarcely dare to express in words, although knowing her character we think we can form a private idea of it, and although a fine womanly soul can think its way into hers and feel with her.

So much is certain, that she had made a firm resolve to do everything that would keep Werther away, and if she delayed, then it was a heartfelt, friendly desire to spare him, because she knew how much it would cost him, indeed that it would be almost impossible for him. Yet she came under greater pressure to act in earnest; her husband said nothing about this relationship, as she too had maintained silence, and she was all the more intent upon proving to him through her actions that her principles were worthy of his own.

On the very day on which Werther wrote the letter to his friend which we have just inserted, it being the Sunday before Christmas, he went to see Lotte in the evening and found her alone. She was occupied with putting in shape some small playthings which she had made up as Christmas presents for her small brothers and sisters. He spoke of the pleasure the little ones would have, and of the times when the unexpected opening of a door and the display of a decorated tree, with its wax candles, candy ornaments and apples, could produce the delights of paradise. "You too," said Lotte, concealing her embarrassment behind a sweet smile, "you too shall have a present, if you are very good: a wax candle and something besides."

"And what do you call being good?" he exclaimed. "How am I to be? How can I be? Dear Lotte!"

"Thursday evening," she said, "is Christmas Eve, and then my children will come here, and Father too, and each one will get his present; come then yourself – but not sooner." Werther was taken aback. "I beg you," she went on, "things are that way, I beg you for the sake of my peace of mind: things cannot, they cannot go on this way." He turned his eyes from her, paced up and down the room, and murmured, "Things cannot go on this way," between his teeth. Lotte, who sensed the terrible state into which these words had plunged him, tried to divert his thoughts by all sorts of questions, but in vain. "No, Lotte," he exclaimed, "I shall not see you again!"

"Why do you say that?" she replied, "Werther, you can, you must see us again, only be moderate. Oh, why must you be born with this vehemence, this unconquerably clinging passion for everything on which you once lay hold! I beg you," she continued, taking him by the hand, "be more moderate! Your mind, your knowledge, your talents, what diverse enjoyments they afford you! Be a man! Turn this unhappy attachment away from a creature who can do nothing but feel sorry for you." He ground his teeth and looked gloomily at her. She held his hand: "Just for a moment, keep a calm mind, Werther," she said. "Don't you feel that you are deceiving yourself, deliberately destroying yourself? And why me, Werther? Just me, the property of another? Just that? I fear, I fear that it is only the impossibility of possessing me that makes this desire so appealing to you." He drew his hand away from hers, looking at her with rigid, angry gaze. "Wise!" he cried. "Very wise! Was it perhaps Albert that made that observation? Diplomatic! Very diplomatic!"

"Anyone can make it," she retorted. "And should there be no girl in the whole wide world to fulfil the desires of your heart? Prevail upon yourself to go in search of one, and I swear to you that you will find her; for I have long been afraid, for you and us, of the limitation which you have imposed upon yourself all this time. Prevail upon yourself! A journey will and must divert your mind! Seek and find a worthy object of your love, and then return, and let us enjoy together the happiness of a true friendship."

"One could have that printed," he said with a cold smile, "and recommend it to all teachers of the young. Dear Lotte! Give me peace for a little while, and all will be fulfilled."

"Only this, Werther, that you do not come here before Christmas Eve!" He was about to reply, when Albert entered the room. They bade each other a frosty good evening, and in embarrassment they walked up and down side by side. Werther began some insignificant conversation, which was soon exhausted; Albert did the same, whereupon he asked his wife about certain commissions, and when he heard that they had not yet been taken care of, he spoke to her some words which seemed to Werther cold and indeed quite harsh. He wanted to leave but could not, and delayed till eight, discontent and anger increasing in him all the while, until the table was set and he took his hat and cane. Albert invited him to stay, but he, in the belief that he was merely receiving an insignificant compliment, returned cold thanks and went away.

He got home, took the candle from the hand of his boy, who was going to light the way for him, and went alone into his room; he wept aloud, talked excitedly to himself, paced vehemently up and down the room, and finally threw himself in his clothes onto the bed, where the servant found him, venturing to enter towards eleven o'clock in order to ask whether he should pull off his master's boots. Werther permitted this then and forbade the servant to enter the room the next morning until he should call him.

Monday morning, the twenty-first day of December, he wrote to Lotte the following letter, which was found sealed on his desk after his death and was brought to her, and which I will insert here a paragraph at a time, in accordance with the writing of it, as revealed by the circumstances.

It is resolved, Lotte, I want to die, and I write this to you without any romantic extravagance, calmly, in the morning of the day on which I shall see you for the last time. When you read this, my dear, a cool grave will already be covering the rigid remains of the restless unfortunate who knows no greater sweetness to fill the last moments of his life than to converse with you. I have had a terrible night, and ah! – a beneficent night. That night has confirmed and fixed my decision: I want to die! When I tore myself away from you yesterday, in the fearful revolt of my mind and with everything rushing to my heart, and I was gripped in chilling horror by my hopeless, joyless existence beside you – I had scarcely reached my room when I flung myself on my knees, beside myself, and you – O God! – granted me the bitterest tears as my last refreshment! A thousand projects, a thousand prospects went storming through my soul, and as last of all the thought stood before me, firm and whole, the last and only one: I want to die! I lay down to sleep, and this morning, in the calm of awaking, that thought still remains firm, still quite strong in my heart: I want to die! It is not despair, it is the certainty that my sufferings are complete, and that I am sacrificing myself for you. Yes, Lotte! Why should I conceal it? One of us three must go, and I will be the one! O my dear! In this torn heart the frenzied thought has slunk about, often – to murder your husband! Or you! Or me! So be it then! When you climb up on the mountain, on some fine summer evening, then remember how I often came up the valley, and then look across towards my grave in the churchyard, and see how the wind makes the tall grass wave back and forth in the rays of the setting sun – I was calm when I began, but now, now I am weeping like a child, since all that is growing so vivid around me.

At about ten o'clock Werther called his servant, and while dressing he told him that he would go away on a journey in a few days, and so he should take out all the clothes and get everything ready for packing; he also gave him orders to ask everywhere for the bills, to bring back some books he had lent and to pay for two months in advance the stipulated amounts to some poor people, to whom he was wont to give something each week.

He had his lunch brought to his room, and after lunch he rode out to see the steward, whom he did not find at

111

home. Deep in thought he walked up and down the garden, seeming to wish to heap upon himself, in this last hour, all the melancholy of recollection.

The little ones did not leave him long in peace, they pursued him, jumped up on him and gave him the news: that when tomorrow, and again tomorrow, and one more day came, they would go to Lotte to get their Christmas presents, and they told him the wondrous things that their little imaginations promised them. "Tomorrow!" he exclaimed. "And again tomorrow! And one more day!" and he kissed them all heartily and was about to leave them, when the little boy asked to whisper something else in his ear. The child revealed to him that his big brothers had written out fine greetings for New Year, so big! And one for Papa, one for Albert and Lotte, and one for Mr Werther too; they were going to deliver them on New Year's Day in the morning. This overwhelmed him, and he gave each of them something, got on his horse, sent good wishes to the steward and rode away with tears in his eyes.

Towards five o'clock he got home and ordered the maid to see to the fire and keep it burning on into the night. He bade the servant pack books and linen into the bottom of the trunk and sew up his outer clothing into a bundle. Thereupon, probably, he wrote the following paragraph of his last letter to Lotte.

You are not expecting me! You thought I would obey and that you would not see me again until Christmas Eve. O Lotte! It is today or never again. On Christmas Eve you will hold this paper in your hand, trembling and wetting it with your precious tears. I will, I must! Oh how happy I feel that I am resolved.

Lotte had meanwhile got into a strange frame of mind. After the last conversation with Werther she had felt how hard it would be for her to part from him, and what he would suffer when he should go away from her.

It had been said in Albert's presence, as if casually, that Werther would not come again before Christmas Eve, and Albert had ridden out to see an acquaintance in the vicinity with whom he had business to transact, and with whom he had to stay overnight.

Now she was sitting alone, none of her brothers and sisters being with her, and abandoned herself to her thoughts, which hovered quietly about her circumstances. She saw herself now united for ever with the husband whose love and loyalty she knew, to whom she was devoted with all her heart, whose calm and reliability seemed veritably destined by Heaven to be such that a good wife might found the happiness of her life upon them; she felt what he would always be to her and her children. On the other hand, Werther had become so dear to her, from the very first moment of their acquaintance the agreement of their souls had shown itself so beautifully, and the long and lasting association with him, together with a number of situations they had gone through together, had made an indelible impression on her heart. She was accustomed to share with him everything of interest which she felt and thought, and his removal threatened to make a breach in her whole being which could never be filled again. Oh, if she could have transformed him into a brother in that moment! How happy she would have been, had it been allowed her to marry him off to one of her friends, and could she have hoped to restore his relation to Albert to all that it had once been!

She had thought over her friends, one after the other, and found something to object to in each one, found none to whom she would not have begrudged him.

Amid all these reflections she only now felt deeply, without making it plain to herself, that it was her secret, heartfelt desire to keep him for herself, and she was saying to herself the while that she could not keep him, might not keep him; her pure, fine, generally light-hearted spirit, so ready to help itself, felt the burden of a melancholy which knows that the prospect of happiness is sealed off. Her heart was oppressed, and a cloud of sadness rested on her eyes.

So it had come to be half-past six when she heard Werther coming up the steps and soon recognized his step and his voice as he asked for her. How her heart beat, and for the first time, we may almost say, at his approach. She would have been glad to refuse to see him, and when he entered she went towards him with a kind of passionate perplexity: "You did not keep your word."

"I promised nothing," was his reply.

"Then at least you should have heeded my request," she responded, "I made it to give us both peace."

She did not rightly know what she was saying, and knew just as little what she was doing when she sent for a couple of her friends so as not to be alone with Werther. He laid down some books which he had brought, asked about others, and now she wished that her friends would come, now that they would stay away. The maidservant came back, bringing word that both asked to be excused.

She was going to have the maid sit in the adjoining room with her work; then she changed her mind again. Werther walked up and down the room, and she went to the piano and began to play a minuet, but it refused to go smoothly. She collected herself and sat down quietly beside Werther, who had taken his accustomed seat on the sofa.

"Have you nothing to read?" she said. No, he had nothing. "In there in my drawer," she began, "lies your translation of some of the songs of Ossian; I have not read them yet, for I always hoped I might hear them from you, but there was never any time or any opportunity." He smiled and fetched the songs, and a shiver went through him as he took them in his hand; his eyes filled with tears as he looked closer at the sheets. He sat down and read.

Star of descending night! Fair is thy light in the west! Thou liftest thy unshorn head from thy cloud; thy steps are stately on thy hill. What dost thou behold in the plain? The stormy winds are laid. The murmur of the torrent comes from afar. Roaring waves climb the distant rock. The flies of evening are on their feeble wings; the hum of their course is on the field. What dost thou behold, fair light? But thou dost smile and depart. The waves come with joy around thee: they bathe thy lovely hair. Farewell, thou silent beam! Let the light of Ossian's soul arise!

And it does arise in its strength! I behold my departed friends. Their gathering is on Lora, as in the days of other years. Fingal comes like a wat'ry column of mist; his heroes are around. And see the bards of song, grey-haired Ullin! Stately Ryno! Alpin, with the tuneful voice! The soft complaint of Minona! How are ye changed, my friends, since the days of Selma's feast? When we contended, like gales of spring, as they fly along the hill, and bend by turns the feebly whistling grass.

Minona came forth in her beauty, with downcast look and fearful eye. Her hair flew slowly on the blast, that rushed infrequent from the hill. The souls of the heroes were sad when she raised the tuneful voice. Often had they seen the grave of Salgar, the dark dwelling of white-bosomed Colma. Colma left alone on the hill, with all her voice of song! Salgar promised to come, but the night descended around. Hear the voice of Colma, when she sat alone on the hill!

COLMA

It is night; I am alone, forlorn on the hill of storms. The wind is heard in the mountain. The torrent pours down the rock, No hut receives me from the rain; forlorn on the hill of winds!

Rise, moon, from behind thy clouds! Stars of the night arise! Lead me, some light, to the place, where my love rests from the chase alone! His bow near him, unstrung: his dogs panting around him. But here I must sit alone, by the rock of the mossy stream. The stream and the wind roar aloud. I hear not the voice of my love! Why delays my Salgar, why the chief of the hill, his promise? Here is the rock, and here the tree! Here is the roaring stream! Thou didst promise with night to be here. Ah! Whither is my Salgar gone? With thee I would fly, from my father; with thee, from my brother of pride. Our race have long been foes; we are not foes, O Salgar!

Cease a little while, O wind! Stream, be thou silent awhile! Let my voice be heard around. Let my wanderer hear me! Salgar! It is Colma who calls. Here is the tree, and the rock. Salgar, my love! I am here. Why delayest thou thy coming? Lo! The calm moon comes forth. The flood is bright in the vale. The rocks are grey on the steep. I see him not on the brow. His dogs come not before him, with tidings of his near approach. Here I must sit alone!

Who lie on the heath beside me? Are they my love and my brother? Speak to me, O my friends! To Colma they give no reply. Speak to me: I am alone! My soul is tormented with fears! Ah! They are dead! Their swords are red from the fight. O my brother! My brother! Why hast thou slain my Salgar? Why – O Salgar! – hast thou slain my brother? Dear were ye both to me! What shall I say in your praise? Thou wert fair on the hill among thousands! He was terrible in fight. Speak to me; hear my voice; hear me, sons of my love! They are silent; silent for ever! Cold, cold are their breasts of clay! Oh, from the rock on the hill; from the top of the windy steep, speak, ye ghosts of the dead! Speak, I will not be afraid! Whither are ye gone to rest? In what cave of the hill shall I find the departed? No feeble voice is on the gale: no answer half-drowned in the storm!

I sit in my grief! I wait for morning in my tears! Rear the tomb, ye friends of the dead. Close it not till Colma come. My life flies away like a dream: why should I stay behind? Here shall I rest with my friends, by the stream of the sounding rock. When night comes on the hill; when the loud winds arise; my ghost shall stand in the blast, and mourn the death of my friends. The hunter shall hear from his booth. He shall fear but love my voice! For sweet shall my voice be for my friends: pleasant were her friends to Colma!

Such was thy song, Minona, softly blushing daughter of Torman. Our tears descended for Colma, and our souls were sad! Ullin came with his harp; he gave the song of Alpin. The voice of Alpin was pleasant: the soul of Ryno was a beam of fire! But they had rested in the narrow house: their voice had ceased in Selma. Ullin had returned, one day, from the chase, before the heroes fell. He heard their strife on the hill; their song was soft but sad! They mourned the fall of Morar, first of mortal men! His soul was like the soul of Fingal; his sword like the sword of Oscar. But he fell, and his father mourned: his sister's eyes were full of tears. Minona's eyes were full of tears, the sister of car-borne Morar. She retired from the song of Ullin, like the moon in the west, when she foresees the shower, and hides her fair head in a cloud. I touched the harp, with Ullin; the song of mourning rose!

RYNO

The wind and the rain are past: calm is the noon of day. The clouds are divided in heaven. Over the green hills flies the inconstant sun. Red through the stony vale comes down the stream of the hill. Sweet are thy murmurs – O stream! – but more sweet is the voice I hear. It is the voice of Alpin, the son of song, mourning for the dead! Bent is his head of age; red his tearful eye. Alpin, thou son of song, why alone on the silent hill? Why complainest thou, as a blast in the wood; as a wave on the lonely shore?

ALPIN

My tears – O Ryno! – are for the dead; my voice for those that have passed away. Tall thou art on the hill; fair among the sons of the vale. But thou shalt fall like Morar; the mourner shall sit on thy tomb. The hills shall know thee no more; thy bow shall lie in the hall, unstrung!

Thou wert swift – O Morar! – as a roe on the desert; terrible as a meteor of fire. Thy wrath was as the storm. Thy sword in battle, as lightning in the field. Thy voice was a stream after rain; like thunder on distant hills. Many fell by thy arm: they were consumed in the flames of thy wrath. But when thou didst return from war, how peaceful was thy brow! Thy face was like the sun after rain; like the moon in the silence of night; calm as the breast of the lake when the loud wind is laid.

Narrow is thy dwelling now! Dark the place of thine abode! With three steps I compass thy grave, O thou who wast so great before! Four stones, with their heads of moss, are the only memorial of thee. A tree with scarce a leaf, long grass, which whistles in the wind, mark to the hunter's eye the grave of the mighty Morar. Morar! Thou art low indeed. Thou hast no mother to mourn thee; no maid with her tears of love. Dead is she that brought thee forth. Fallen is the daughter of Morglan.

Who on his staff is this? Who is this, whose head is white with age? Whose eyes are red with tears? Who quakes at every step? It is thy father, O Morar! The father of no son but thee. He heard of thy fame in war; he heard of foes dispersed. He heard of Morar's renown; why did he not hear of his wound? Weep – thou father of Morar! – weep; but thy son heareth thee not. Deep is the sleep of the dead; low their pillow of dust. No more shall he hear thy voice; no more awake at thy call. When shall it be morn in the grave, to bid the slumberer awake? Farewell, thou bravest of men! Thou conqueror in the field! But the field shall see thee no more; nor the dark wood be lightened with the splendour of thy steel. Thou hast left no son. The song shall preserve thy name. Future times shall hear of thee; they shall hear of the fallen Morar!

The grief of all arose, but most the bursting sigh of Armin. He remembers the death of his son, who fell in the days of his youth. Carmor was near the hero, the chief of the echoing Galmal. Why bursts the sigh of Armin, he said? Is there a cause to mourn? The song comes, with its music, to melt and please the soul. It is like soft mist that, rising from a lake, pours on the silent vale; the green flowers are filled with dew, but the sun returns in his strength, and the mist is gone. Why art thou sad – O Armin! – chief of sea-surrounded Gorma?

Sad! I am! Nor small is my cause of woe! Carmor, thou hast lost no son; thou hast lost no daughter of beauty. Colgar the valiant lives, and Annira fairest maid. The boughs of thy house ascend, O Carmor! But Armin is the last of his race. Dark is thy bed, O Daura! deep thy sleep in the tomb! When shalt thou awake with thy songs? With all thy voice of music?

Arise, winds of autumn, arise; blow along the heath! Streams of the mountain roar! Roar, tempests, in the groves of my oaks! Walk through broken clouds, O moon! Show thy pale face, at intervals! Bring to my mind the night, when all my children fell; when Arindal the mighty fell; when Daura the lovely failed! Daura, my daughter! Thou wert fair; fair as the moon on Fura; white as the driven snow; sweet as the breathing gale. Arindal, thy bow was strong. Thy spear was swift in the field. Thy look was like mist on the wave; thy shield, a red cloud in a storm. Armar, renowned in war, came, and sought Daura's love. He was not long refused: fair was the hope of their friends!

Erath, son of Odgal, repined: his brother had been slain by Armar. He came disguised like a son of the sea: fair was his skiff on the wave; white his locks of age; calm his

*serious brow. Fairest of women, he said, lovely daughter
of Armin! A rock not distant in the sea, bears a tree on its
side; red shines the fruit afar! There Armar waits for Daura.
I come to carry his love! She went; she called on Armar.
Nought answered, but the son of the rock, Armar, my love!
My love! Why tormentest thou me with fear? Hear, son of
Arnart, hear: it is Daura who calleth thee! Erath the traitor
fled laughing to the land. She lifted up her voice; she called
for her brother and her father. Arindal! Armin! None to
relieve your Daura!*

*Her voice came over the sea. Arindal my son descended
from the hill, rough in the spoils of the chase. His arrows
rattled by his side; his bow was in his hand: five dark-grey
dogs attend his steps. He saw fierce Erath on the shore: he
seized and bound him to an oak. Thick wind the thongs
of the hide around his limbs; he loads the wind with his
groans. Arindal ascends the deep in his boat, to bring Daura
to land. Armar came in his wrath, and let fly the grey-
feathered shaft. It stung; it sunk in thy heart. O Arindal my
son! For Erath the traitor thou diedst. The oar is stopped
at once; he panted on the rock and expired. What is thy
grief, O Daura, when round thy feet is poured thy brother's
blood! The boat is broken in twain. Armar plunges into the
sea, to rescue his Daura, or die. Sudden a blast from the hill
came over the waves. He sunk, and he rose no more.*

*Alone, on the sea-beat rock, my daughter was heard to
complain. Frequent and loud were her cries. What could
her father do? All night I stood on the shore. I saw her by
the faint beam of the moon. All night I heard her cries.
Loud was the wind; the rain beat hard on the hill. Before
morning appeared, her voice was weak. It died away, like
the evening breeze among the grass of the rocks. Spent with
grief, she expired, and left thee Armin alone. Gone is my
strength in war! Fallen my pride among women! When the
storms aloft arise; when the north lifts the wave on high; I
sit by the sounding shore, and look on the fatal rock. Often*

by the setting moon, I see the ghosts of my children. Half-viewless, they walk in mournful conference together.

A flood of tears, which burst from Lotte's eyes and gave her oppressed heart relief, checked Werther's reading. He threw down the papers, seized her hand and wept the bitterest tears. Lotte rested her head on the other hand and hid her eyes with her handkerchief. Both were in a fearful agitation. They felt their own wretchedness in the fate of those noble souls, felt it jointly, and their tears united. Werther's lips and eyes were aglow on Lotte's arm; a shudder seized upon her; she tried to withdraw, yet pain and sympathy lay upon her like lead, laming her. She took a deep breath for her recovery, and begged him, sobbing, to continue, begged with all the force of Heaven in her voice. Werther trembled, his heart ready to burst, and he lifted the paper and read half brokenly:

Why dost thou awake me, breath of spring? Thou wooest me, saying, "I bedew thee with the drops of heaven!" But the time of my wilting is near, near is the blast that will strip me of my leaves! Tomorrow the wanderer will come; he that saw me in my beauty will come; his eyes will seek me everywhere in the field, and will not find me...

The whole force of these words descended upon the unhappy man. He flung himself down before Lotte in the fullness of despair, seized her hands, pressed them into his eyes and against his brow, and a premonition of his terrible intention seemed to flit through her soul. Her senses grew confused, she pressed his hands, pressed them against her breast, bent down with a sorrowful movement to him, and their glowing cheeks touched. The world was lost to them. He flung his arms about her, pressed her to his breast and covered her trembling, stammering lips with frenzied kisses. "Werther!" she cried with stifled voice, turning away from him. "Werther!" – and with feeble hand she pushed his breast from hers – "Werther!" she cried with the composed accents of the noblest dignity. He did not resist, released her from his arms, and cast himself down senselessly before her. She drew herself up, and in alarmed confusion, quivering half in love, half in anger, she said, "That is the last time! Werther! You will not see me again." And casting a glance of the fullest love upon the wretched man, she hurried into the adjoining room and locked the door behind her. Werther stretched out his arms towards her, but did not venture to restrain her. He lay on the floor, his head on the sofa, and in this position he remained for more than half an hour, until a noise brought him to. It was the maid, who was about to set the table. He paced up and down the room, and when he again found himself alone he went to the door of the cabinet and called in a low voice, "Lotte! Lotte! Just one word more! A farewell!" She was silent. He persevered and pleaded and persevered; then he tore himself away and cried, "Farewell, Lotte! For ever, farewell!"

He came to the city gate. The guards, who had long grown used to him, let him out without a word. There was a light drizzle half between rain and snow, and it was nearly eleven when he rapped again. His servant observed, when Werther got home, that his master's hat was missing. He did not venture to say anything, but helped him undress and found everything wet. Later, his hat was found on a cliff which overlooks the valley from the slope of the hill, and it is inconceivable how he climbed it on a wet, dark night without falling.

He laid himself down in bed and slept long. The servant found him writing when he brought him coffee the next morning at his call. He was writing the following portion of his letter to Lotte.

For the last time, then, for the last time I open these eyes. They are, alas, not to see the sun any more, for a dreary, misty day is keeping it concealed. Well, then mourn, Nature! Your son, your friend, your beloved is approaching his end.

Lotte, this is a feeling without compare, and yet it is closest to a half-conscious dream, to say to oneself, "This is the last morning." The last one! Lotte, I have no feeling for that word "last". Am I not standing here in my full strength? And tomorrow I shall lie outstretched and limp on the ground. Die! What does that say? Look, we are dreaming when we speak of dying. I have seen many a man die, but mankind is so hemmed in that it has no feeling for the beginning and end of its existence. As yet, still mine and yours! Yours, O beloved! And in a moment – separated, parted – perhaps for ever? No, Lotte, no – how can I perish? How can you perish? Why, don't we exist? Perish! – what does that mean? That is again just a word! An empty sound! without anything for my heart to feel. Dead, Lotte! Interred in the cold ground, so confined! So dark! I had a friend who was everything to my helpless youth; she died, and I followed her corpse, and stood at the grave as they let the coffin down, and the ropes rolled down beneath it with a humming sound, and came up again with a rush, and then the first shovelful of earth rattled down, and the frightened lid gave out a dull sound, and duller and ever duller, and at last was all covered! I flung myself down beside the grave – moved, shaken, terrified, my innermost being rent apart, but I did not know how I felt – how I shall feel – Die! Grave! I do not understand the words!

Oh forgive me! Forgive me! Yesterday! It should have been the last moment of my life. O you angel! For the first time, for the first time without any doubt my inner, inmost being was permeated with the glow of the rapturous feeling: she loves me! She loves me! On my lips the sacred fire is still burning that flowed out from yours, and new, warm rapture is in my heart. Forgive me! Forgive me!

Oh, I knew that you loved me, knew it from your first soulful glances, from the first pressure of your hand, and yet, when I was away from you again, or when I saw Albert at your side, I was again despondent in feverish doubts.

123

Do you recall the flowers that you sent me after you were unable to say a word to me in that wretched company, or extend your hand to me? Oh, I knelt before them half the night, and they gave me the assurance of your love. But alas! those impressions passed by, as the feeling of God's grace gradually retreats once more from the soul of the believer, though it had been bestowed upon him with all the fullness of heaven in a sacred and visible symbol.

All that is transitory, but no eternity shall extinguish the glowing life which I tasted yesterday on your lips, which I feel in my soul now! She loves me! This arm has embraced her, these lips have quivered on her lips, this mouth has stammered words on hers. She is mine! You are mine! Yes, Lotte, for ever.

And what of the fact that Albert is your husband? Husband! That would be for this world, then – and for this world a sin that I love you, that I would like to draw you out of his arms into mine? Sin? Very well, and I am punishing myself for it; I have tasted it in all its heavenly ecstasy, that sin, have drawn into my heart the elixir of life and strength. From that moment you are mine! Mine, O Lotte! I shall go before you! Go to my Father, to your Father. To him I will make my complaint, and he will comfort me, until you come, and I will fly to meet you and clasp you and abide with you in the sight of the Infinite One in eternal embraces.

I am not dreaming, I am in no delusion! When nearing the grave my inner light increases. We shall be! We shall see each other again! And see your mother! I shall see her, shall find her, ah, and pour out my whole heart to her! Your mother, your image.

Towards eleven, Werther asked his servant if Albert had perhaps returned. The man said, yes, he had seen his horse being led away. Thereupon his master gave him an unfolded note with this written on it:

*Would you kindly lend me your pistols for a journey I have
in mind? May all go well with you!*

The sweet woman had slept little during the night; what she
feared was now decided, and decided in a manner which she
could neither have surmised nor feared. Her blood, which was
wont to course so purely and freely, was in a feverish turmoil,
and a thousand warring feelings rent her noble heart. Was
it the fire of Werther's embraces that she felt in her bosom?
Was it anger at his presumptuousness? Was it a mournful
comparison of her present condition with those other days
of wholly candid, untrammelled innocence and carefree
confidence in herself? How should she meet her husband? How
confess to him a scene which she might so easily confess, and
yet which she did not dare to confess? They had maintained
a mutual silence for so long, and should she be the first to
break the silence and make so unexpected a disclosure to her
husband at an inopportune time? She was already afraid that
the mere report of Werther's call would make an unpleasant
impression on him, and now there was even this unexpected
catastrophe! Could she rightly hope that her husband would
see it in quite the right light, and accept it wholly without
prejudice? And could she wish that he might read in her soul?
And then again, could she dissemble before the man to whom
she had always been like a glass of bright crystal, open and
clear, and from whom she had never concealed, never been
able to conceal, any of her feelings? Whatever she thought
of doing, it caused her concern and made her uneasy; and
again and again her thoughts reverted to Werther, who was
lost to her, whom she would not give up, whom she, alas!
must abandon to himself, and to whom, when he had lost her,
nothing more would be left.

How heavily lay upon her now – a thing which at the moment
she could not make clear to herself – the burden of the barrier
which had developed between them! Sensible and good as they
were, they began to observe silence towards each other with

respect to certain hidden differences, each one feeling right on his side, wrong on the other, and circumstances became so complex and so critical that it was impossible to disentangle things at the decisive moment on which everything depended. Had a happy confidingness brought them closer together again, sooner, had love and indulgence come to life mutually between them, causing their hearts to open, perhaps our friend might still have been saved.

One more strange circumstance must be added. Werther, as we know from his letters, had never made a secret of his longing to quit this world. Albert had often opposed this, and at times Lotte and her husband had talked about it. The latter, seeing that he felt a decided repugnance to such an act, had very often indicated, with a kind of irritation which was otherwise quite foreign to his character, that he had much cause to doubt the seriousness of such a resolve, and he had even allowed himself an occasional jest on the subject, and had imparted his disbelief to Lotte. This quieted her on the one hand, to be sure, when her thoughts presented such a sad picture to her mind, but on the other hand she felt herself prevented thereby from communicating to her husband the anxieties which were torturing her at that moment.

Albert returned, and Lotte went towards him with an embarrassed haste; he was not cheerful, his transaction had not been completed, for he had found the neighbouring bailiff to be a stubborn, petty person. Moreover, the bad roads had made him peevish.

He asked whether anything had happened, and she replied overhastily that Werther had been there on the previous evening. He asked whether letters had come, and received the answer that letters and some parcels were in his room. He went there, and Lotte remained alone. The presence of the man whom she so loved and honoured had made a new impression upon her heart. The thought of his nobility, his love and kindness, had brought more calm to her spirit, she felt a secret impulse to follow him, and she took her work and went to his room, as she was frequently wont to do. She found him occupied in opening the parcels and reading the letters. Some seemed not to have the most agreeable contents. She put some questions to him which he answered curtly, then he went to the desk to write.

So they had been together for an hour, and in Lotte's soul the darkness kept deepening. She felt how hard it would be for her to disclose to her husband, even if he were in the best of moods, what she had on her heart; she lapsed into a melancholy which became the more frightening to her as she sought to conceal it and to check her tears.

The entrance of Werther's servant brought her embarrassment to the highest pitch; he handed the note to Albert, who turned calmly to his wife and said, "Give him the pistols." – "I wish him a happy journey," he said to the lad. This struck her like a thunderbolt, and she staggered to her feet, not knowing what she was doing. Slowly she went over to the wall, with trembling hand she took down the weapons, wiped off the dust and hesitated, and she would have delayed still longer if Albert had not hurried her with an enquiring look. She handed the unhappy instruments to the boy without being able to utter a word, and when he had left the house she folded up her work and went to her room in a state of the most inexpressible uncertainty. Her heart predicted to her all possible terrors. Now she was on the point of flinging herself at her husband's feet and disclosing everything to him, the story of the preceding evening, her guilt and her premonitions. Then again she saw no way out of her difficulty, and least of all could she hope to persuade her husband to go to Werther. The table was set, and a good woman friend who only came to ask a question and was going to leave at once – and remained – made the conversation at table endurable; they controlled themselves, they chatted, they related things, they forgot themselves.

The lad came back to Werther with the pistols, and the latter took them from him with delight upon hearing that

Lotte had handed them to him. He had bread and wine brought, bade the lad go and eat, and sat down to write.

They have passed through your hands, you wiped the dust off them, and I kiss them a thousand times, for you touched them, and you, spirit of heaven, favour my resolve! And you, Lotte, hand me the instrument, you, from whose hands I have wished to receive my death, and, ah! receive it now. Oh, I asked my lad about everything. You trembled as you handed them to him, you spoke no farewell! Woe! Woe! No farewell! Should you have locked your heart against me, for the sake of the moment which attached you to me for ever? Lotte, not in a thousand years can that impression be effaced! And I feel that you cannot hate him who has such a glowing love for you.

After eating, he bade the lad complete the packing, tore up papers, went out and took care of some small bills. He came home again, went out again, passed through the gate, heedless of the rain, went into the count's park, roved further around the countryside, came back as night was falling, and wrote the following.

Wilhelm, for the last time I have seen fields and woods and sky. Farewell to you, too! Dear mother, forgive me! Console her, Wilhelm! God bless you both! My affairs are all in order. Farewell! We shall see each other again, and more happily.

I have rewarded you ill, Albert, and you will forgive me. I have disturbed the peace of your house, I have brought distrust between you. Farewell! I will end it. O that you two might be made happy by my death! Albert! Albert! Make that angel happy! And so may God's blessing abide with you!

That evening he did much rummaging among his papers, tore up many of them and threw them into the stove, and sealed some packets addressed to Wilhelm. They contained short essays and detached thoughts, a number of which I have seen. At ten o'clock, after he had had more fuel put on the fire, and had a bottle of wine brought, he sent the servant to bed, whose bedroom as well as those of the domestics were far to the rear; the lad lay down in his clothes so as to be on hand early in the morning, for his master had said that the post horses would be at the house before six.

Past Eleven

All is so still about me, and my soul so calm. I thank you, God, for granting me in these last moments this warmth, this strength.

I step to the window, dear one! and look out, and even through the passing, flying storm clouds I see single stars of the eternal sky. No, you will not fall! The Eternal bears you on his heart, and me. I saw the stars in the handle of the Great Wain, the most loved of all the constellations. When I used to leave you at night and walked out of your gate, it would be facing me. With what intoxication I often gazed at it! often with upraised hands made of it a symbol, a sacred marker of my present blessedness! And even now – O Lotte, what does not remind me of you? Do you not surround me? And have I not like an insatiable child snatched and kept all sorts of trifles that had felt your sacred touch?

Dear silhouette! I bequeath it back to you, Lotte, and beg you to honour it. Thousands, thousands of kisses I have pressed upon it, a thousand times I have waved to it, when I went out or came home.

I have written your father a note asking him to protect my corpse. There are two linden trees in the churchyard, in a rear corner towards the fields; there I wish to rest. He can and will do that for his friend. You ask him too. I will not demand from pious Christians that they should lay their bodies next to a poor unfortunate. Oh, I wish you would bury me by the roadside, or in the lonely valley, so that priest and Levite should bless themselves as they passed the stone marker, and the Samaritan should drop a tear.

Here, Lotte! I do not shudder to seize the cold and terrible cup from which I am to drink the intoxication of death! You handed it to me, and I do not quail. All! All! Thus all the desires and hopes of my life are fulfilled! So coldly, so rigidly to knock at the brazen portal of death.

That I could have gained the happiness of dying for you! Lotte, to offer myself up for you! I would die courageously, I would die joyously, if I could restore to you the peace and the rapture of your life. But alas! to few noble souls is it given to shed their blood for their dear ones, and by their death to enkindle a new, hundredfold life for their friends.

In these clothes, Lotte, I wish to be buried, for you have touched them, hallowed them, and I have made this request of your father. My soul is hovering over the coffin. Let no one search my pockets. This pale-pink bow which you wore on your bosom, the first time I found you among your children – oh kiss them a thousand times and tell them of the fate of their unhappy friend. The dear ones! They are swarming around me. Ah, how I attached myself to you! and from the first moment could never let you go! This bow is to be buried with me. On my birthday you gave it to me! How I drank in all those things! Ah, I did not think that the way would lead me to this! Be calm! I beg you, be calm! –

They are loaded – the clock strikes twelve! So be it, then! Lotte! Lotte! Farewell! Farewell!

A neighbour saw the flash of the powder and heard the shot, but as all remained still, he gave it no further attention.

At six in the morning the servant steps in with a light. He finds his master on the floor, finds pistols and blood. He calls, he takes hold of him; no answer, only a death rattle. He runs for the doctors, runs to Albert. Lotte hears the bell pulled, and trembling seizes on all her limbs. She wakes her husband, they get up, crying and stammering the servant tells his news, and Lotte drops in a faint at Albert's feet.

When the physician reached the unhappy man, he found him on the floor, not to be saved; his pulse was still beating, his limbs were all paralyzed. Over his right eye he had shot himself through the head, brains had oozed out. Uselessly, they opened a vein in his arm; blood flowed, and he was still drawing breath.

From the blood on the arm of the chair it could be inferred that he had done the deed while sitting at the desk; then he had slumped down, rolling convulsively around the chair. He lay on his back, powerless, towards the window, fully dressed and booted, in the long blue coat with the yellow waistcoat.

The house, the neighbourhood, the town got into a turmoil. Albert entered. They had laid Werther on the bed with bandaged brow; his face was already like that of a dead man, and he did not move a muscle. There was still a fearful rattle in the lungs, now weak, now stronger; his end was expected.

Of the wine he had drunk only one glass. *Emilia Galotti** lay open on the desk.

Let me say nothing about Albert's consternation and Lotte's grief.

The old steward came on a gallop at the news, and kissed the dying man amid burning tears. His older sons soon followed him on foot, dropped down beside the bed, expressing the most uncontrollable grief, and kissed his hands and his mouth, and the oldest, whom he had always loved the most, clung to his lips until he had expired and they tore the boy away by force. At twelve noon he died. The presence of the steward and the measures he took quelled a commotion. At night towards eleven he had him buried at the spot Werther had chosen. The steward followed the body, and his sons, but Albert found it impossible. There were fears for Lotte's life. Workmen carried him. No clergyman escorted him.

Notes

p. 9, *Melusine and her sisters*: In European medieval legend, Melusine was a fairy, half-woman half-fish. Goethe's parallel may be an allusion to the fact that in some sources she is described as the protector of the magical Fountain of Thirst.

p. 12, *from Batteux... classical antiquity*: Charles Batteux (1713–80) was a French philosopher whose treatises on aesthetics in art and literature were widely read. The politician, travel writer and classical scholar Robert Wood (1716/17–71) was most famous, especially in Germany for his influential *Essay on the Original Genius and Writings of Homer*, published posthumously in 1775. Roger de Piles (1635–1709) was an influential French art theorist, whose writings were pivotal in their defence of genius and individual expression in the face of rigid classical rules. Johann Winckelmann (1717–68) was an important art historian, who set the foundations for the study of ancient Greek art and whose Hellenistic ideals greatly contributed to Neoclassicism in art and literature. The Swiss theologian and philosopher Johann Georg Sulzer (1720–89) was the first to publish a systematic general theory of the arts in the German language. Christian Gottlob Heyne (1729–1812) was a renowned classical philologist and lecturer.

p. 14, *Wahlheim*: The reader will save himself the trouble of looking for the places mentioned here; it has been found necessary to change the true names given in the original text. (GOETHE'S NOTE) "Wahlheim" means roughly "home of one's choice".

p. 22, *she answered...*: It has been found necessary to suppress this passage in the letter, in order to give no one any occasion for complaint. Although, ultimately, no author can care much about the judgement of an individual girl and an unstable young man. (GOETHE'S NOTE)

p. 23, *about...*: Here too the names of some native authors have been omitted. Whichever of them enjoys Lotte's approval will surely feel it in his heart if he should read this passage, and of course no one else needs to know. (GOETHE'S NOTE)

p. 27, *Klopstock... ode*: Klopstock's poem in free rhythms, 'Die Frühlingsfeier' ('The Festival of Spring'), had a sensational appeal in eighteenth-century Germany.

p. 29, *Penelope's impudent suitors*: *Odyssey* xx, 251.

p. 30, *Except ye become as little children*: Matthew 18:3.

p. 33, *combated ill humour from the pulpit*: We now have an excellent sermon on this by Lavater, among those dealing with the Book of Jonah. (GOETHE'S NOTE) Johann Kaspar Lavater (1741–1801) also wrote a work on physiognomy, to which Goethe contributed.

p. 38, *the prophet's never-failing cruse*: 1 Kings 17:14–16.

p. 54, *the fable... death*: In a fable of Jean de La Fontaine (1621–95) the horse, unable to outrun the deer, asks man's help.

p. 54, *my birthday*: Goethe was born on 28th August.

p. 58, *you*: Albert addresses her as *Sie*, not *du*, thus bearing out Werther's observation of Albert's deep respect for her.

p. 67, *bronze age*: The allusion is to Ovid's four ages of man. The bronze age is one's forties and fifties; the iron age embraces the last quarter of a normal life.

p. 69, *private letter*: Out of respect for this excellent man, the above-mentioned letter has been withdrawn from this collection, as well as another which is referred to later on, because it was not thought that such an indiscretion could be excused even by the warmest gratitude of the reading public. (GOETHE'S NOTE)

p. 85, *Kennicott, Semler and Michaelis*: The English theologian Benjamin Kennicott (1718–83) was one of the foremost textual critics of the Bible. The German theologian Johann Salomo Semler (1725–91) advocated the critical textual analysis of scripture rather than interpreting Biblical writing as the literal word of God. Johann David Michaelis (1717–91) was well-known Biblical scholar and expert on Hebrew antiquity.

p. 131, *Emilia Galotti*: A tragedy by G.E. Lessing, which was found open beside the body of the young man whose suicide moved Goethe deeply and was one of the motivations for *Werther*.

ONEWORLD CLASSICS

ONEWORLD CLASSICS aims to publish mainstream and lesser-known European classics in an innovative and striking way, while employing the highest editorial and production standards. By way of a unique approach the range offers much more, both visually and textually, than readers have come to expect from contemporary classics publishing.

~

To order any of our titles and for up-to-date information about our current and forthcoming publications, please visit our website on:

www.oneworldclassics.com